ACCOLADES FOR ELISA LORELLO'S BOOKS

"With a confident, chatty writing style, Elisa Lorello has created witty, amusing, realistic characters in *Faking It*."
~ Alice Osborn, N.C. author, musician, and teacher

"Alternating narration keeps the story lively, while the protagonists' authentic struggles and aspirations will keep readers rooting for them until the last page."
~ Publishers Weekly, for *Adulation*

"Lorello, a native Long Islander like both Danny and Sunny, gives her readers the gift of two hilarious yet grounded protagonists, whose romance lends truth to what people say about love: 'sometimes you just know.'"
~ Booklist, for *Adulation*

"A romantic, delicious romp! Heartfelt and full of humor, it will leave you hungry for more."
~ Gail Simmons, food critic, TV host and author of "Talking with My Mouth Full," for *Pasta Wars*

"Authors Elisa Lorello and Craig Lancaster have crafted a charming update on the classic romantic comedy with *You, Me & Mr. Blue Sky*. Honest, heartwarming, and wickedly funny, this is one love story you won't want to miss."
~ Karen McQuestion, author of *Hello, Love*

"I loved *Friends of Mine*! Elisa Lorello perfectly captures the specialness of growing up Duranie in the awesome '80s. But *Friends of Mine* isn't just for the 'Duran Duranged'; it's for fans in general. If the longest (and best?) relationship you've ever had is with a band—or a sports team, or an actor, or a writer—then this book is for you."
~Lori Majewski, Sirius XM radio host and co-author of *Mad World*

Also by Elisa Lorello

The Faking It series
Faking It
Ordinary World
She Has Your Eyes
Faked Out
Love, Wylie

Standalones
Why I Love Singlehood
Adulation
Pasta Wars
The Second First Time
Big Skye Littleton
You, Me & Mr. Blue Sky

Memoir
Friends of Mine: Thirty Years in the Life of a Duran Duran Fan

Awards and honors

She Has Your Eyes: finalist, International Book Awards

You, Me & Mr. Blue Sky: finalist, 2019 International Book Awards; finalist, 2020 Best Book Awards

ALL OF YOU

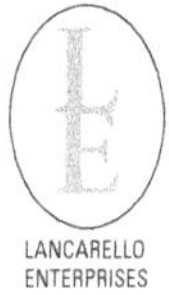

LANCARELLO
ENTERPRISES

ALL OF YOU

a novel

ELISA LORELLO

This is a work of fiction. Names, characters, places, and incidents either are the product of the author's imagination or are used fictitiously. Any resemblance to actual events, locales, organizations, or persons living or dead, is entirely coincidental and beyond the intent of either the author or the publisher.

Lancarello Enterprises
1219 Frost Street
Billings, MT 59105

Lancarello Enterprises softcover ISBN-13: 978-0-9976433-5-0

Printed in the United States of America

0 9 8 7 6 5 4 3 2 1

"What I want to know is why there aren't more female producers."—John Taylor, bassist of Duran Duran

"It all comes down to what happens between the notes." —Mike Lorello, musician, producer, engineer, and the best big brother anyone could want

This book is for them.

PROLOGUE

Of all the iconic venues to play at around the world, my favorites are—and in some cases, were—in New York.

Shea Stadium. Yankee Stadium. Madison Square Garden.

And my number one favorite, Radio City Music Hall. Although I have to admit, Madison Square Garden is a close second.

I can't put my finger on why Radio City Music Hall, in particular, does it for me. It could be its ninety-year-old history and art deco design—the majestic grand foyer, the large and lavish auditorium, the lofty mezzanines—interwoven with my own history. It was where my Uncle Oscar took me to see a screening of *Beatlemania* when I was eight years old, then promptly took me out because the pot smoke was stifling (and… working). It was where my parents took me to see the Rockettes when I was ten and complained about everything from our seats ("too far"), to the performance ("a disappointment"), to even the concessions at intermission ("someone needs to learn how to mix a drink"). It was where I saw my first rock concert at fourteen years old (the Go-Go's and INXS), and where I was the second time I saw Taro, at fifteen years old. (The first time? Madison Square Garden, of course.)

And it was where I headlined my first solo, sold-out concert. April 1, 1987. I was six months into my Sweet Sixteen.

My second and final performance at Radio City Music Hall was in 1988, with, believe it or not, INXS. It was a shared billing, but I was seen as a warm-up act, and frankly that was OK with me. I had come full circle.

Incidentally, Radio City Music Hall was also the last place I saw the love of my life. Literally and figuratively.

There was a time when I couldn't bear to set foot in the lobby. But thirty years later, I was back on the Radio City Music Hall stage, and it was almost as if not a day had passed since I'd last been there. And yet, I felt no heartbreak, no grief, no regret. Instead, I felt at home. The electric magic was palpable—the fans, most of whom had grown up with us, breathed it in and blew it back to us with their chants and cheers and singing and shouting. And we absorbed it, soaking it into our skin and feeling it invigorate our bodies. There was no better medicine, no safer high, no brighter sunshine. No other moment of aliveness that you would want to spend eternity in.

I hadn't realized how much I'd missed it. But there I was, performing with my band.

No. *Our* band. Garrett and Gavin Chandler and Michael Spaulding and Ian Bensa and Johnny Rogers. And me, Johanna Parker, formerly known as Paisley Parker.

I play the drums.

CHAPTER ONE

If I hear that damn song one more time, I'm going to strangle someone with a G-string. The guitar kind, that is.

I'd been hearing "Glossy" everywhere—the diner, the supermarket, "Throwback Thursday" during lunch hour on the pop radio stations, and, of course, the new Cover Girl lip gloss TV commercial.

This morning, I heard it in the coffeeshop I've been patronizing ever since it took over the old Italian deli's location. It's my routine: up at seven a.m., walk two miles outside or on the treadmill, drive over for coffee and a muffin, then back home and straight into the studio. Coffee and a muffin may not be a good post-exercise breakfast, but aside from having little interest in cooking (although I'm not bad at it), the truth was that without my coffee run—and not the drive-thru window—I probably wouldn't leave the house or interact with humans face-to-face. Besides, I find coffee and a muffin a simple pleasure.

The woman in front of me bopped her head just as the second chorus of "Glossy" ended and the breakdown began. She stepped up to the counter, shook herself out of her musical nostalgia, and placed her order with her name: Melissa.

"Sorry," she said with a giggle. "I love this song. It takes me way back."

Out of reflex, I tapped the air at the precise beat of the orchestral sample at the end of the breakdown. Melissa noticed and laughed. "I can see you like it, too," she said.

I don't know why, but every time I'm in a position where I feel a twinge to disclose the truth, a second impulse muzzles me. "Glossy" was a number one hit for three weeks straight in 1986. I wrote and sang and co-produced it all before my sixteenth birthday. Played most of the instruments, too. Heck, it even won a Grammy for Best Single that year, and the album, *Next Wave*, went gold and earned a nomination for Best Album. I was Long Island's darling. Thirty-five years later, that song still puts food on my table.

In other words, nothing to be ashamed of.

But still.

Cherry, the new barista (there was always a new barista), rolled her eyeballs. "It's on rotation so I hear it, like, a million times a day. I kind of hate it now."

I stared at the floor and exhaled an exaggerated, elongated breath. I mean yeah, I was sick of it, too, but that didn't make it *hate*-worthy.

"I'll bet that would drive me crazy, too," said Melissa.

"It's just so…stupid," said Cherry. "I mean, who wrote those lyrics?"

"I did," I blurted.

Shit.

Melissa and Cherry looked at me, perplexed. "Did what?" they asked in unison.

"I wrote it. And recorded it. It's my song. That's me. Paisley Parker."

God, how I loathed that name.

Melissa narrowed her eyes. You know, the what-is-a-famous-eighties-teen-pop-star-doing-in-a-coffeeshop-in-Manhasset look. Cherry didn't seem to give a rat's ass.

"Are you punking me?" Melissa asked.

I held up two fingers as if glued together. "Scout's honor."

"Prove it," she dared.

"Can I take your order first?" Cherry asked me, her impatience conspicuous.

I placed my order, stepped aside, closed my eyes, and sang the final verse following the breakdown and the bridge, doubling my adolescent vocal near perfectly. Sounded good, actually. Maybe I should have doubled the vocals back then.

I could sense the other patrons turning their heads in my direction. When I opened my eyes, instead of impressed or delighted faces, I saw bewildered gawks. Instead of applause, I heard the whirrings and stirrings of the coffeeshop.

My cheeks burned.

I could read Melissa's mind: *No way is* the *Paisley Parker standing in front of me.* And in a way, she was right. Paisley Parker was never the real me, and I never quite lived up to her. Melissa peered at me intently, trying to find some semblance of familiarity with my former self—pudgy cheeks covered with stark slashes of blush, the moussed shock of bleached blonde hair, the salmon pink paisley scarf that matched my lip color, the stonewashed blue denim jacket, the scrunchy socks over leggings and a spandex skirt with salmon pink high-tops to match—and instead she found dark circles under tired eyes, product-free ash brown hair with gray skunk stripes on the top and sides like Lily Munster, pulled back in a ponytail; blue jeans and Sketchers and a well-worn peacoat. It was a sharp contrast not only to Paisley but also to Melissa, who was outfitted in business attire and a stylish trenchcoat, a messenger bag slung across her shoulder, her auburn hair smoothed into a flawless french braid.

"You don't look anything like Paisley Parker," she declared.

"I lost thirty-some pounds and aged thirty-some years," I said amiably. She remained wary.

"What are you doing *here*?" she asked.

"I live nearby," I replied.

"What do you do now?"

"I'm a producer and a sound engineer, mostly."

After a beat of silence, I tacked on, "Of music."

Another beat.

"I still make albums. Except they're other people's now."

She looked at me, dumbfounded, as if she needed additional explanation, or perhaps further proof that I was who I claimed to be. Or maybe she was unimpressed. "Producer and engineer" was nowhere near as sexy as "pop star." Even "former pop star" has a little ring to it.

This was why I never opened my mouth. I couldn't stand that look of disappointment. Of incredulity. Of *pity.* Poor Paisley. Look what you've become.

To my relief, "Glossy" ended and INXS's "Devil Inside" took the baton. There's an album I wish I'd made. Every part of it is perfection. Should I tell Cherry that the stereo speakers were poorly positioned in the store, and thus weren't doing Michael Hutchence justice? Nah. Nothing she could do about it.

A second barista, Josh, placed Melissa's cup on the

counter and called out her name. She grabbed the cup and turned to me.

"Well, good luck to you," she said in a tone used to placate unruly children. "Nice meeting you."

"You, too," I said.

No request for an autograph or a selfie. I was equal parts relieved and disappointed, as I often am.

Cherry looked at me. "So that really was your song?"

"Really was," I said. *Still is.*

"Were you, like, a one-hit wonder?"

Before I had a chance to respond, Josh called my name—*Joey*—even though he knew me, and Cherry moved on to the next patron.

"Thanks, Josh," I said as I took my goods. I overheard Josh say as I left, "Wow, she's been coming in here all this time and I never knew she used to be famous."

Time to get a new coffeeshop, because you can't show your face in there anymore. Seriously, what were you thinking? Don't ever do that again.

I drove home in silence, but that hook stayed between my ears, in stereo.

I touch your glossy lips
I feel your glossy skin
I see your glossy smile
I need to make you mine.

Cherry was right—the lyrics weren't exactly those of Van Dyke Parks or Neil Finn. But, hey, I was fifteen and in love. I wrote what I knew. They're indelibly eighties, indelibly adolescent, and indelibly pop. And they were true.

Besides, that drum sound is as killer today as it was thirty-five years ago. Took us two days and ten microphones to get that sound.

You should be proud.

What sucks more—missing the thing you love, or missing the love you had for it in the first place?

CHAPTER TWO

As I pulled into the driveway, I clicked the remote garage door opener, A patch of snow at the edge of the front lawn stubbornly refused to melt even though spring was a week away. The grass had yet to turn green and demand its own care; the garden had been barren for years.

Car parked and breakfast in tow, rather than use the garage entrance to the house, I stepped outside, lowered the door with the keypad, and walked along the brick path past the south side of the house. The sage green paint of the façade was faded and whispering for a new coat. I unlocked and passed through the gate, ambled around to the back, and down the steps to the private entrance. I kept the path clear of snow and de-iced it during the winter for clients, but the bricks were cracking, and I made a mental note to call someone next month.

Entering my recording studio this way rather than trudging

through the house was my version of pretending I went to an office like everyone else; not that such a thing mattered to anyone. Unlocking the door and dismantling the alarm, I entered the control booth and set the tall iced coffee and the blueberry muffin and napkins on the mix desk. Next, I removed my coat and fingerless gloves, tossed them on an empty chair to my right, and sat at the desk, turning on both Mac screens. I'd recently switched the desktop screen wallpaper to a grainy photo of Gav and me on the infamous staircase inside Abbey Road studios, taken when I was twenty years old. Hallowed ground. As if the DNA of every note the Beatles ever sang and played and recorded there remained preserved in the walls and floors, like a sarcophagus. And if you just touched those walls, your skin would absorb this DNA, it would become a part of you, and you'd be able to infuse it into every note you put forth from then on.

I missed that magic. I missed believing in it.

Or maybe I was missing Gav again.

The cream-painted wall behind the mix desk served as a gallery and timeline of my accolades: gold and platinum records first as Paisley Parker, performer, then as Joey Parker, producer. Me on the cover of *Rolling Stone* in December 1986, sporting a red-and-green paisley scarf and a furry Santa hat and posing with a red-and-white stocking as tall as I was, overflowing with presents. "What Paisley Parker Wants for Christmas," spelled in bold, sans serif typeface underneath. An assortment of framed *Billboard* chart lists from 1986 to 1989 with my singles in the Top Five—"Glossy," "Too Good to be True," "Oyster Bay," and a remake of Carole King's "I Feel the Earth Move" that went to number three, bested only by Johnny Hates Jazz and George Michael. *Billboard* lists of singles and albums I'd worked on as producer or engineer that also charted. Framed photos of me receiving the Best Single Grammy, presenting at the 1987 MTV Video Music Awards, performing at *Dick Clark's New Year's Rockin' Eve* in 1988. Photos of me with Prince. With Janet Jackson. With Jon Ravelle and Edgar Naturally.

On the left corner of the mix desk sat a photo of me with Uncle Oscar, taken just after I signed my first album contract with Capitol Records. Uncle Oscar, now eternally forty-five years old, and I were both beaming; yet while I was smiling for the camera, his attention was on me, eyes glimmering with pride, as if I were his own child. (And for all intents and purposes, I was.) Didn't matter that he was almost completely bald and fifty pounds overweight. He was vibrant. He was free. He was floating. If only I knew then how little time he had left.

Were there a fire and everything perished, including the hundreds of thousands of dollars of studio equipment, I think I would be most upset to lose that photo.

I hadn't worked in at least a month. The last record I did was for a Montauk DJ named Matty B, a seven-minute mashup of a house groove with a funky Nile Rodgers-style guitar riff in E flat. I used a custom Fender Stratocaster and doubled it with a synth—and the only lyric was a breathy, seductive hook of "Get busy. Get funky. Get on the floor and dance." I mixed it, too. Matty still hadn't paid me for it, but according to him, the feet hit the hardwood from the very first beat and have continued to do so with every spin. Last I heard, word had spread and other DJs got hold of it, in Manhattan and even as far away as Miami.

At least I still had the Midas touch, even if that gold wasn't landing in my pockets.

Thanks to the Cover Girl contract and a few other licensing

deals in the past couple of years (Uncle Oscar's final gift to me was a lawyer to revert and retain the publishing rights to my Paisley Parker catalogue), I've been able to keep the electricity on, the studio running, and my belly full. Yet I wondered if even licensing would be sustainable in the coming years, given the current state of the music business. Streaming services like Spotify had cut into royalties so drastically that it wouldn't matter if I had another hit as big as "Glossy." YouTube's ubiquity had taken the rest.

Retirement age was still some fifteen years away, and even though I'd secured financial stability for my sixties and beyond, what would or could I do in the meantime? What job prospects did a single, soon-to-be-fifty-year-old lifelong musician, producer, and engineer with no college degrees or office skills have?

"Teach," suggested my friend Rick Smitts two weeks ago. In a career spanning almost forty years, Rick had worked his way from assistant engineer in a private recording studio to senior engineer at the former Electric Lady studio (of Jimi Hendrix fame) to executive engineer with Columbia Records, now owned by Sony. These days, he was on the lecture circuit at music colleges and conferences across the country to promote his memoir, *Behind the Desk*, a tell-all of stories about some of the biggest albums of the 1990s. "Five Towns Music College would take you in a heartbeat," he said. "In fact, I know the dean there. I'll give you his number."

Perhaps I could pay my experience and expertise forward. But would there be a music business for these kids to graduate to?

"Or join me on the circuit," he said. "You'll probably get more gigs than I do. A female engineer and producer? Audiences will eat that shit up."

"They haven't so far," I said.

After a beat, Rick tried again. "You could go back on the road."

"As what—a legacy act?"

"Why not? Plenty of eighties nostalgia festivals, fairs, even cruises."

"I'd have to revive Paisley again, wouldn't I?"

"Is that so bad?" he asked.

"I'd rather not," I replied.

Rick gave up. "Well, you're not lacking options. Or excuses," he tacked on.

He wasn't wrong.

With the free time, I'd been trying to write and record a few songs of my own. Compared with most of my night owl colleagues, I was more of a lark, doing my best work in the morning and early afternoon. When I worked with clients, however, I often scheduled the sessions in the evening to accommodate their peak performance and productivity. And I kept a lot of caffeine on hand.

I sipped my iced coffee through the straw as I booted up Pro Tools on the Mac and opened the files for "Shit Song," a working title that was living up to its name. I'd been tinkering with the melody all week, trying desperately to find the spark, the hook, the passion. Isolating the bass track I'd laid down yesterday, I listened to it and made some adjustments with the faders on the mixing console; what was once a hulking desk full of knobs and switches and lights and faders was now reduced to a digital replica on a computer screen and operated by a mouse, yet it yielded the same results.

I restarted the song and listened to it with the rest of the tracks—drums, guitar, and a simple keyboard arrangement. No vocals; I hadn't yet written lyrics.

Technically, it was good. Emotionally, however, it wasn't grabbing me, wasn't beckoning me to bob my head like Melissa at the coffeeshop, wasn't making me *feel* anything.

Maybe that's why hearing "Glossy" was irritating me so much lately. Not because I'd moved on but rather because, deep down, I was afraid I'd *not* moved on. The process had been smooth as butter back then—crafting a song was like baking and layering a cake, all the ingredients working together—and I had loved every minute of it.

Had hindsight distorted the memory? Was it really easier back then? Wasn't I supposed improve with age? How could I have written such a monster hit at age fifteen and not be able to find the pleasure groove at age forty-nine?

Besides, even if a few new songs had potential, what was I going to do with them? I had no record label, no management, and no more clout in the music business as a feature act.

I altered the synthesizer part so that it was less brassy.

Added a new piano line.

Put a compressor on the cymbals.

Overdubbed the bass guitar, locking it to the bass drum.

An hour later, I listened to the entire work in progress, start to finish.

It was a good song.

But it wasn't a hit. It wasn't magic.

It wasn't *me*.

What was missing?

Maybe it really was time to quit. Retire early. I could sell the house. Sell the studio and all my gear. Move off the Island and head south, where there was a lower cost of living and less snow. Atlanta had ascended in recent years.

I stared at the waveforms on the computer screen.

Remember the days before digital? Remember smoky

studios and all-night mix sessions? Remember reel-to-reel tape machines and the those mammoth mix desks? Remember the challenge to squeeze twenty-four tracks on a four-track recorder, like George Martin and Geoff Emerick had to do on the Beatles' Sgt. Pepper's Lonely Heart's Club Band*?*

Music isn't fun anymore.

The realization was a gut punch. I couldn't remember the last time I had fun. The last time I experienced joy, pure elation. The last time I felt challenged. The last time I felt like part of something bigger than myself.

I couldn't remember the last time I didn't feel lonely.

First you crave to be known. Then you crave to be alone. Then you crave to be remembered. Then you crave to be alive.

That's what was missing.

CHAPTER THREE

The following morning, although I resumed the walking and coffeeshop rituals (drive-thru this time), I skipped the studio and surveyed each room in my house, legal pad and pen in hand, listing what needed decluttering, upgrading, repairing, repainting, and/or replacing. I'd closed on the four-bedroom, three-bathroom house just after my eighteenth birthday, when I was officially and legally free of my parents. Although I'd never envisioned myself having a family, Port Washington seemed like a good location for not only a residence but also a recording studio; it was close enough to access Manhattan (the Long Island Rail Road station was reasonably close) but far enough away to maintain a modicum of privacy. Plus fellow musicians could stay in one of the three additional bedrooms if they wanted or needed to. And over the years, some had.

"Make sure you take care of your future," Uncle Oscar had advised after *Next Wave* went gold. "Don't get caught up in fancy boats and cars and toys. Think long term. Buy real estate. Keep your equipment current. Put cash away for retirement. You're in a feast-or-famine business. You could last one year or ten, and it has nothing to do with your talent."

He was right, as usual, and I still thank him for it. In addition to the house, my only splurge had been on an interior designer; she had selected stylish yet practical furniture, paint, and décor. I also hired a crew to transform the unfinished basement into a state-of-the-art recording studio with private entrance for clients—the basement space had been the most appealing feature of the house, plus the small, low-maintenance acreage.

My home improvement to-do list was less about vanity and more about improving resale value. Over the years, I'd updated and upgraded here and there, but it hadn't been enough. And yet, I wasn't sure I wanted to pull that trigger. For the past thirty years, this house had been the one constant in my life, a sanctuary and refuge. It had kept me safe. Kept me sheltered. Kept me independent.

Or perhaps it had caged me all these years. Sure, I came and went as I pleased, but why had I never ventured farther? Why had I never traveled? Not toured, but *traveled.* Why had I isolated myself like this?

After lunch, I returned to the studio. Stood in its heart center and took in the panorama, starting with my drum kit and moving to the multiple stands cradling the Stratocaster and Rickenbacker electric guitars, Hofner bass guitar, and Epiphone acoustic guitar, all designed for the left-handed player. To its right, a double-rack of classic Yamaha and Roland synthesizers. And next to that, several microphones on stands awaiting a singer. Strategically placed speakers and amps and monitors completed the setup.

God, how I revered this room. I loved the smell of metal and wire cables and nickel and nylon guitar strings, the feel of the floors as I tapped out a beat, the sight of every instrument. Hell, I could practically taste every song that had ever been born here.

And of course, the music—beginning as a thought or an emotion, a picture or a story, and transforming into a glorious, golden sound.

I then returned to the control booth, sat at the mix desk, refreshed the computer screen, and checked my email inbox. Among the spam and direct marketing ads for studio gear and software and my invoices that went unacknowledged was an email with a Dropbox attachment from Rick. I was just about to read it and open the attachment when the phone rang. I looked at the caller ID and picked up the receiver.

"Ricky," I said in lieu of "hello." "I was just about to call you."

"Did you get it?" he asked.

"I'm looking at it as we speak. Haven't opened it yet. What is it?"

"The original multitrack files to that Taro album that bombed in 2011. Don't ask how I got them," he said with a devious chuckle.

"What Taro album?" I asked.

"You never heard of it?"

Then it came to me: *Been Too Long.* I had bought it at the time but never brought myself to listen to it.

"Forgot about it, actually," I said.

Rick knew I'd preceded my music career as a Taro teeny-bop fan. In fact, anyone who'd read that *Rolling Stone* article about me back in the day knew; I'd confessed as much.

"It was a master of suck, Joey," he said. "Timmy Tonka produced."

I squinched my face as if I'd just sucked a lemon peel. I'd forgotten that, too. Pairing Taro with Timmy Tonka was like pairing a filet mignon with Kool-Aid. I meant no disrespect to Timmy Tonka (or Kool-Aid), but the two just didn't go together.

"Christ," I said.

"It was the only way Warner would sign them. Tried to appeal to a younger audience and draw in some new fans, I suppose. Pissed off the die-hards something fierce."

"I can imagine," I said.

"How is it that you, the mega-fan, didn't know?" he asked.

"I took down the bedroom posters a *loooong* time ago, Rick."

"Well, give these a listen. They're all there. The entire album."

"I have a lot of free time these days, so I might as well. Thanks, man."

"Anytime, friend."

"Which reminds me—the reason I was going to call…" I started. "You still have the contact information of that college dean?"

"Sure," he said. "I'll send it to you." He paused for a beat. "You've had enough?"

"I think so, yes."

"They'll be lucky to have you. Seriously, Joey, you'll do great as an instructor. They'll probably let you design your own curriculum. You're so versatile. It's a no-brainer to hire you. Plus, they could probably use some estrogen, you know what I'm saying?"

I never knew how to take such a comment. I knew Rick meant to be complimentary, but it always felt backhanded. To the industry and the world, I was never just a producer and engineer; I was a *female* producer and engineer.

"At least it's a steady paycheck," I said.

Ugh. Something about those words: *steady paycheck.* They dropped in the pit of my stomach like rocks. Being a musician had paid me in lots of ways, but "steady paycheck" was never a word or a thing I'd associated with it. I hadn't had one of those since I'd worked for Uncle Oscar's store back in my early teens. I'd long forgotten how it was done.

"Beats digging a hole," he replied.

"Very true," I said. "Thanks. And thanks for the tracks."

"My pleasure. Have fun."

I returned the phone to its cradle. Sixty seconds later, Rick's email with the Five Towns College contact information appeared. I clicked on it, read its contents, and jotted it on a legal pad next to me.

I stared at what I just scribbled.

Then I looked at Gav and me at Abbey Road.

Next, Google. I typed "taro been too long" into the search box while the files transferred from Dropbox to Pro Tools. Scanned through the search results, consisting mostly of reviews and social media links.

"Taro Fails to Connect with Old and New Audiences," read a *Billboard* headline.

"Taro Should Have Predicted this Flop," said *People* magazine.

Consumer reviews ranged from "The band's fuck-you to its fans" to "It's just not the same without Gav" to "I loved this new direction and think their fans need to grow up."

Typically, I don't like to read reviews of anything I haven't yet listened to because I don't want them to cloud my judgment, but I was already biased when it came to Taro. They were my generation's Beatles—teen idols with exceptional musical talent—except they commercially crashed and cratered by the end of the 1980s, as did others who had ridden the MTV wave. And like so many bands whose lives were tragically cut short (literally, in Taro's case), the wondering of what might have been surpassed the awe of what they really were.

Before I dove into to the files Rick sent, I scanned my digital downloads library and found the album. I wanted to listen to the finished product, although I knew that it wouldn't necessarily give me a sense of the band's intention. I'd experienced it many times—an album could end up very different from what you'd originally envisioned. Any number of factors could be at play—writer's block, choice of recording venue (not just studio, but city), chemistry among the artist and the producer and the record label, and so on.

I also clicked on and inspected the *Been Too Long* album cover art: no band photo—just a London subway tunnel with a wide-angle shot of a train zooming ahead. The same spot where the five band members posed for their 1982 self-titled debut album. Now fully down the Taro rabbit hole, I clicked on that cover art next and ogled each band member, all adorned in black leather pants and striped shirts with bandanas and scarves and colorful suede ankle boots that only guys as pretty as they were could pull off. Those were the post-punk, post-New Romantic days, but their hairstyles were still coiffed with burgundy and blue dye framing their chiseled cheekbones. They were all in their mid to late teens, yet they'd looked like they were in their early twenties. Their follow-up mega-smash album two years later, *Fortune Tellers*, featured a spread of five tarot cards, each band member's likeness replacing the traditional medieval images. They wore neon seersucker suits with their ties tucked into their shirts, their faces less pale than the previous cover and more success-stamped. They were tanned, their hair fantastically frosted in shades of blonde and bronze and orange.

Die-hard fans knew the original band name had been Tarot, but bassist and band co-founder Garrett Chandler didn't want people to pronounce it as Ta-ROT or Ta-ROW, but rather as TARROW, rhyming with "arrow." (Of course, most people called them TAR-ow, rhyming with "car-bo.") Garrett's twin brother, Gavin, the other founder as well as the drummer, had preferred the look of the bookended T's, but the rest of the band voted audial aesthetic over visual.

Fortune Tellers officially put Taro on the musical map. In fact, they'd taken over the world.

Of course, the teenage me had fallen for their looks; I was still a girl, after all, even if I opted for Wrangler jeans and cowboy boots over Daisy Dukes shorts and Dr. Scholl's sandals. However, as always, the music had hooked me first. While my best friend Laurel danced around her bedroom, singing into her hairbrush, I planted myself on the floor of my bedroom, plugged my headphones into the stereo, and listened for every nuance of melody and harmony and rhythm. I listened to *Fortune Tellers* first with the left speaker turned down, then again with the right speaker turned down, and again after tinkering with the treble and bass levels, just like Uncle Oscar had told me he'd done the first time he'd listened to *Sgt. Pepper's Lonely Hearts Club Band.*

A year later, when I rented a studio to record my own album, I played *Fortune Tellers* full blast, sitting at the mix desk perfectly positioned between the wall-mounted speakers, and practically had a religious experience. Garrett and Gavin Chandler had worshipped at the altars of Brian Wilson and Jeff Lynne and Phil Spector and had produced something so clean and precise, yet something so upbeat and danceable and refreshing. And *different*. And they were so *young*. Nothing about the album sounded derivative, yet there was a bit of repurposing. It was as if David Bowie and David Cassidy had a love child.

If Carole King's *Tapestry* and The Bee Gees' *Saturday Night Live* soundtrack and the Beatles' everything hadn't already done it, those first two Taro albums sealed my fate as a career musician and producer.

Back in the present, I leaned back in my aeronautic chair—the queen's throne, I called it—and punched up *Been Too Long*. One thing that sucked about digital content: no liner notes. I'd have to go back to Google to determine who engineered and mastered the album, whether Timmy Tonka brought in additional musicians, and where the band had recorded it.

To say the album was an assault on my ears would be too harsh, but it certainly didn't make a positive first impression.

First of all, the programmed drum loops. Every freaking song, and not the slightest variation on any of them. Gav's absence was painfully and audibly conspicuous. I understood why they'd gone this route, but there was no way he would he have approved. For God's sake, try reverb! Overdubs. A little compression on the high hat, perhaps.

Second, lead singer Ian Bensa's vocals were overprocessed, and not in a good way. There was no need to auto-tune Ian (his bandmates called him "Benny," according to the teen magazines back in the day) other than to perfect the pitch, although his slightly off-key style had always given the songs a bit of a crooner quality. This heavy-handed bit of sound engineering just made Ian sound downright inauthentic.

A producer, first and foremost, must serve the needs of

the song. Timmy Tonka had come on the scene as a DJ in the late 1990s, known mostly for dance club remixes of pop and hip-hop singles. I had no problem with the genre, and the one time I'd met him after a performance with none other than Matty B. at a nightclub, he was friendly enough. But he had no patience for sound quality. Turn up the volume and the bass—that was his calling card. Give it a good beat (although clearly he'd phoned that one in on this album). Timmy was also known to be a bit of a control freak, which must have set Garrett Chandler off.

Overall, the problem wasn't the songwriting. The songs were good. Or rather, they could have been good had they been placed in the hands of someone who understood Taro, their history, and their style. What should have been ballads were set to beat boxes. What could have been good ol' pop songs sounded like watered-down dance club records.

Taro was as eloquent as Electric Light Orchestra, but they were also as funky as Chic. They were precise, but they were also playful. And they had been a captivating live band. You couldn't go to a Taro concert and leave without floating back home. It wasn't just a live performance—it was an experience of aliveness. Breathing and beating.

Put another way, it was musical magic.

Been Too Long was none of those things. No wonder the fans revolted. Poor Gav must have turned over in his grave. Ditto for Edgar Naturally, rest his soul, the engineer mostly responsible for the definitive sound of Taro's classic catalogue and one of my heroes.

After listening to the entire album, I opened the files Rick sent me. Fourteen songs in all, three of which had never made it to the album but had been used as B-sides. One by one, I punched up the multiple tracks of each song, isolating them, working the digital faders to manipulate and improve each instrumental contribution.

I started with the drums, of course. With a couple of clicks of the mouse, I pulled up the EQ panel and amended the percussion on the first song, "Login." A little reverb on the snare, and a bit of depth to the kick drum without quite so much low end. With a few additional clicks, I accessed a file housing a voluminous library of drum samples and proceeded to accessorize the loop with strategically placed high hat and toms fills.

I replayed the song with the revised drum tack. Already it had more dimension, made me sit up in my seat a little more upright.

In fact, I felt a spark.

Hmmmmmmmm.

Screw the drum loop altogether. Let's start over.

I left the control booth and padded to my drum kit, picked up the sticks patiently resting on the snare, and pumped the track into the room via remote control. I then rerecorded the track with live drums.

It was close to midnight by the time I finished overhauling "Login." The next day, I gave the tongue-in-cheek "Slow Burn" a makeover, remixing Ian's vocals, which were quite marvelous in their original form, and lowering Garrett's bassline an octave. And although I'd tossed out Michael Spaulding's keyboard parts altogether (I couldn't believe he'd done them at all—they sounded nothing like his signature style), I replaced them with what had been his go-to synthesizer in the 1980s, a Yamaha DX-7, for a retro sound.

I didn't even need coffee to boost my energy.

By the end of the week, I finished three songs and sent them to Rick, subject heading: *This is all your fault.* I also decided to send them to Laurel—it had been weeks since she and I had caught up, and she was still a devout Taro fan. She would appreciate that I gave her a little "inside scoop." The subject heading for her email was *FYEO: for your ears only.*

And then something crazy happened.

CHAPTER FOUR

Rick called me a few days later, irked. "Geezus, Joey, what the hell?"

"What's wrong?" I asked.

"They're on YouTube."

"What's on YouTube?"

"The remixes."

I was still slow on the uptake. "What remixes?"

"*Your* remixes, Joey. The *Been Too Long* remixes."

Rick's words finally kicked in. Whacked me. Like getting pummeled in dodge ball.

I stood up. "WHAT?"

"How did they get there? I know *you* didn't do it."

Laurel.

Laurel had called me about an hour after I had emailed her the remixes.

"Ohmigod, I cannot believe you got to do a Taro remix and didn't tell me!" she said, barely leaving space between the words, just like the way we used to speak when we gushed over Garrett, Gavin, Ian, Johnny, and Michael. I had introduced Laurel to Taro when I heard their very first single, "Crush," on the radio station WLIR (which was always one step ahead of the mainstream stations), but she had MTV and introduced me to their videos—and thus, their faces. "I thought they broke up years ago," she said.

"Well, I didn't exactly 'get' to do it," I replied. "No one commissioned it. My buddy Rick sent me the files, and I did it for fun."

"Wait—this isn't official? They're not releasing this?"

"No. You and my buddy Rick are and will be the only ones who have heard it."

"What? No. Joey, they're too good. You should send them to the band."

"I should not," I said.

"Why not? They're even better than the original versions. You don't think they'll love it?"

"I think they'd be insulted."

Especially Garrett.

"Why?"

"Because it's upstaging them. Imagine if you did your job and then someone walked into your office after you left, fixed everything you did wrong, then shoved it in your face."

Laurel disagreed with the analogy. "This is your problem, Jo-Jo. You don't value yourself. Taro needs to hear this. The fans need to hear this. You need to network yourself."

"No, no, and no," I said.

"It's because of Gav, isn't it?"

I rubbed my eyes wearily. "Laurel, not this again."

"I know you loved him, but it was a long-distance relationship at best," she said.

It was a lot more than that.

"Look, I did the remixes because I had some free time, and I sent them to you because I knew you'd appreciate it," I said. "Just don't play them for anyone, OK?"

"Do you know the last time I heard real music? First it was 'Wheels on the Bus.' Then it was *Frozen*. Now it's stuff I've never even heard on the radio. I don't even have to buy it for the girls; they listen to it all online."

Precisely why I was making plans for an early retirement.

Laurel and I had been friends since elementary school, in Mrs. Metzger's second-grade class, where our desks were paired. Her long, flaxen hair, smooth as cornsilk, contrasted my boyish brown, Dorothy-Hamill-gone-wrong haircut. Whereas she dressed in rainbow shirts and purple T-shirts with iron-on unicorns, my mother took me clothes shopping once a year and refused to cater to the trends. My Aunt Mary Lou was more understanding in that regard, and she often bought me trendier clothes for Christmas and my birthday, or even holidays like Easter and Valentine's Day.

Laurel loved to bake. I loved to drum. She was a planner and an organizer. I was a thinker and a daydreamer.

I envied Laurel in every way. She was pretty and popular and seemed to fit in wherever she went. Sometimes I didn't know why she even liked me at all. But we were inseparable after school and on weekends, riding bikes together, playing board games, and spending our allowances on earrings or stickers or stuffed animals at the mall. We both had big dreams—to be the best we could be at the things we loved to do. And when Taro came along, we dreamed even bigger and grew even closer.

Until my single and album came out and soared to number one, and I left home and school to tour. When Laurel graduated from high school, she went to college; I bought a house. After that, she got married; I became a full-fledged producer and engineer. She had kids; I had songs. She had a dog; I had a treadmill. Laurel's life had become about schlepping her daughters to Girl Scouts, soccer, after-school dances, tutoring, their grandparents' houses, the movies, and a zillion other things that made my head spin. And that was all with a full-time job as an administrative assistant. I couldn't fathom having that life. It was like trying to imagine living in a foreign culture with a different language and customs. And yet, it was important for me to maintain our friendship, to remember what I—what *we*—had been like before Paisley Parker and paparazzi and growing up so fast. And I still envied Laurel. She still fit in.

"Remember," I had said at the end of our call. "Don't tell anyone about the remixes, except maybe Bill." (Her husband.)

"I won't," she'd promised. "Love you."

"Love you," I replied. "Kiss everyone for me."

I mentally replayed my conversation with Laurel in a matter of seconds while still on the phone with Rick.

"I'll take care of it," I told him, not outing Laurel as the one who leaked the remixes, especially since I had yet to find out for sure.

"I don't think you can," he said.

"Well, shit," I said. "I'll figure something out and call you back, OK?" We exchanged goodbyes and I hung up, pausing for less than a second before I dialed Laurel.

She answered with, "Don't be mad at me, Jo."

"What part of *for your ears only* did you not understand?"

"I made an executive decision. They needed to be heard by more than just you and me."

"It wasn't your decision to make, Laurel. There were other people involved. People who could get into trouble."

Laurel all but ignored that last part. "Look, I'm really sorry for going behind your back, but have you seen how many views it's gotten on YouTube already? Like, ten thousand hits, plus a whole bunch of likes and shares from my social media pages. And I tagged you and Taro on everything. Not to mention I went scrolling on *their* social media pages and a bunch of people have posted it and tagged them. And not a bad word yet."

Laurel might as well have posted a photo of me drunk and naked. I rubbed my temples. There was no way to put the pin back in this grenade.

"I appreciate your intentions, Laurel. I really do. It's just... you still shouldn't have done it."

She became quiet and contrite. "I just...I just want you to have the fame and recognition you had when 'Glossy' first came out. You deserve that."

"I've had a lot of success since then," I argued. "Just because it was behind the desk with other people's music doesn't mean it wasn't my success, too."

"Yes, but...it's not the same."

Nothing was the same.

"I'm sorry for scolding you, and I know your heart was in the right place," I said. "Thank you."

"I'm sorry it caused such a problem for you," she said, her tone laced with hurt.

"We'll get together soon, OK?"

Neither of us believed it. We exchanged awkward goodbyes.

I dialed Rick again. “I’m sorry, man,” I said. “I sent them to an old friend who’s also a longtime Taro fan. Should’ve told her to keep a lid on them.” It seemed only fair that I take the bullet for her. “I never mentioned your name or involvement, though.”

“It’s OK,” he said. “I mean, there’s nothing that can be done about it now.”

“Should I be flattered that they’ve gone viral?”

“They were smokin’,” Rick offered.

“Now what?” I asked.

“Wait for your phone to ring, I guess.”

CHAPTER FIVE

Sure enough, around ten o'clock Monday morning, I was in the kitchen when I heard the phone in the studio ring. I raced downstairs and picked it up just before the call diverted to voicemail.

"Parker Studio, Joey speaking," I said between panting breaths.

"Is this Johanna Parker?" asked a female voice in a British accent.

"It is," I replied.

"I'm Janet St. James from Roman Entertainment. We represent the band Taro."

And here comes the cease-and-desist order.

"Yes," I said, playing it cool.

"Garrett Chandler would like to set up a meeting with you. I see on your website that you're located on Long Island. Would you be able to meet with him in East Hampton tomorrow?"

Garrett still had a house in East Hampton? Damn, I really was out of the loop.

"Let me check my schedule," I said, rustling the computer mouse and looking at nothing but the Abbey Road photo. "Sure, I think I can move some things around. What time?"

We agreed upon one o'clock. I wondered: Was Garrett sitting next to her while this call was taking place? Perhaps listening on another line? It didn't sound like I was on a speakerphone.

We exchanged thank-yous and good-byes.

Tomorrow. One o'clock. Me and Garrett Chandler in the Hamptons.

I hoped it would go better than the last time we were in a room together.

CHAPTER SIX

Long Island is just that—a long island. Technically, it's a peninsula. I'm embarrassed to say I learned that from a clue on *Jeopardy!*, many years after a teenage Laurel argued that it was and I vehemently insisted it wasn't. I still double down, despite what Laurel and *Jeopardy!* say. It's an island. It's also a juxtaposition of urban and rural and affluence and poverty and ocean and pine barrens. Of commerce and respite. The farther you get away from Manhattan and mayhem, the closer you get to vineyards and vacations.

I had considered buying a house in the Hamptons shortly after my second album, *Mindfield*, went to number seven on the *Billboard* pop chart. But I'd had the foresight to assume that I'd need relatively easy access to Kennedy and LaGuardia airports. And if I was going to be a producer one day, I would probably be working in Manhattan, and who would want *that* commute? Not to mention that when I built a studio, artists wouldn't have to trek all the way out to the East End. Plus, I could visit Uncle Oscar and Aunt Mary Lou in Dix Hills, or so I'd thought. No way I could have predicted that Uncle Oscar was going to die so young, or that Aunt Mary Lou would move to Florida so soon after his death.

And yet, maybe I should have bought a beach cottage back then. A place to escape. Indulged just a little bit.

The drive to East Hampton from Port Washington took approximately two hours, the skies sunny and the eastbound traffic on the Long Island Expressway scarce. I drove without music or an audiobook, but my thoughts were noisy and restless and flitted from subject to subject.

For instance, I spent several miles obsessing about my outfit. My wardrobe wasn't versatile. The invitations to parties and awards shows had dried up decades ago, and after I lost weight, I'd donated my gowns and high-fashion pieces to thrift stores. I'd attended the Audio Engineering Society conference in the city a couple of years ago and found myself overdressed and self-conscious in a business-style skirt and jacket. And I hated wearing skirts, even when I was a little girl and a teenager. Today, I settled on tan corduroys with distressed ankle-length boots, and a white poplin button-down shirt. I even put on makeup and styled my hair. Because as much as I couldn't stand to admit it, I didn't only want to look presentable—I also wanted to look *attractive*, if not pretty. This was still Taro, after all. And Garrett and Gavin Chandler had been the most attractive of the quintet, even if Garrett had never thought the same of me. He'd even gone out of his way to say so. *That night.*

I tried not to think about what Garrett wanted to discuss with me, or what I would say when I came face to face with him for the first time in more than twenty-five years. However, my brain rolled out several scenarios: Me in staunch defense of the remixes getting out on YouTube (*"It wasn't me. I was hacked."*). Or me in staunch defense of the remixes themselves. (*"Friends don't let friends use drum loops."*) Me being defensive in general. (*"You could have just sent me the cease-and-desist letter. I don't know why you had to summon me all the way out here. At least I can stop at the Golden Pear on the way back."*)

Or perhaps me telling off Garrett Chandler once and for all.

By the time I'd gotten off Montauk Highway, I not only couldn't remember having driven thus far—highway hypnosis—but also lacked any cohesive train of thought. The GPS directed me via a female English accent (a little like Janet St. James, come to think of it) even though the area was somewhat familiar to me. When I pulled up to the thick, wrought iron entrance gates, the house and property hidden by towering evergreen shrubbery, I rolled down the window, leaned out, and pushed the security button. Seconds later, a buzzing sound activated the mechanized doors and they opened slowly, as if luring me to an execution rather than a meeting with one of the latter twentieth century's biggest worldwide pop stars. My aging Honda looked downright scruffy as I parked it next to a salsa red convertible BMW; it was an older model but as pristine as if it had just been driven off the lot. Seeing it conjured an image of a teen magazine cover featuring Gav and Garrett in matching Taro tour shirts and stonewashed jeans, splayed across the hoods of their sleek black Beamers nose-to-nose, identical in every way, smiling cheekily. You could tell they were close, that they reveled in their twinship. Read each other's minds and finished each other's sentences and probably felt each other's physical pains long distance. Could tell that they were best friends. Laurel and my junior high school friend Jessica, a Garrett fan, and I had detailed plans of our double wedding to Gav and Garrett—because of course we assumed they would insist on a double wedding. Laurel, of course, would be my matron of honor, having already married Ian. Funny how immature and embarrassing such fantasies are once you're sharing the stage with them—literally—and creepy when, years later, you find out some of the fantasies boys *and* girls had about you.

Also odd when your fantasy pretty much comes true, only to be torn off you like a bandage.

I exited the car and my boots clacked on the asphalt from the driveway to the slate path that led to wide, red-hued double doors and weathered cedar shingles—a classic East End beach house look. The Atlantic Ocean roared behind it, and I inhaled the scent of salty surf. I almost expected one of those huge knockers on the Munster's house from the classic 1960s sitcom, making the same thundering sound. Instead, I pressed a tiny doorbell.

A golf-ball-sized lump of anticipation bounced between my throat, chest, and stomach as I tapped my foot in nervous rhythm (200 beats per minute, I surmised) and waited for someone to open the door.

And waited.

With every passing second that the door remained closed, the golf ball morphed into pliers squeezing my organs.

Just as I rang the bell a second time, the door whooshed open.

Garrett Chandler.

He was barefoot, dressed in ripped jeans and a black button-down shirt poorly hiding a slight paunch. His hair, once thick and plush and silky chestnut frosted with blond streaks, was dark with shocks of gray at the temples, much like my own, slightly receding from his forehead striped with frown lines. The alabaster face from music videos and magazine pinups was now somewhat sallow, with a visible scar of a long-ago gash running along the bottom of his chin below a five o' clock shadow. His topaz-blue eyes had faded to more of a gray, the way the ocean looks on a cloudy day.

He was four years my senior, but he looked even older than that.

Garrett Chandler, the charming, cocky, teenage heartbreaker and eligible bachelor, could've been a model had the music thing not worked out (and an argument could've been made that it hadn't), was a mere mortal. Even I had to adjust to that home truth, after all these years.

For chrissakes, he could've at least put on socks and shoes for me. And shaved.

And yet, something about him was still captivating. Seeing him was like seeing a ghost. Was this what Gav would have looked like by now, but with more light and life in his eyes, more sparkle? Would he and I have been living in this house, or one like it?

I swallowed hard and averted my gaze—Garrett's presence elicited not only the what-if but also the what-really-happened. In an instant, I relived it all—every ugly word and intentionally inflicted pain and emotional shrapnel.

Garrett smirked more than smiled. "Paisley Parker. Blimey, you lost a lot of weight. I wouldn't have recognized you if I bumped into you in the street," he said in a British accent with traces of American dialect. He seemed both amiable and sullen, more the former than the latter.

"I go by Joey now," I said as he stepped aside to let me in. "And I could say the same about you. Looking unrecognizable,

I mean." I wasn't intending to be combative, yet I could hear the sharpness in the words as I said them.

He closed the door behind us.

"I didn't know you still had a house out here," I said, willing my nerves to settle as I eyed the hardwood floors throughout the foyer and the rooms in sight.

"The very one we bought thirty years ago, or however long it's been."

We. I knew whom *we* referred to.

He continued. "Kept it all these years. Moved in permanently about ten years ago, I think. The sound of the surf is a better sedative than all that shit I was addicted to, so it's good for me. Plus, you know, private. C'mon, I'll give you a tour."

"I live up-island," I said as I followed him out of the foyer.

"I know," he called back.

My skin tingled. *You know? For how long have you known?*

He led me from room to room on the main floor, high ceilinged and sparsely decorated, pointing out specific features here and there. I spoke at a volume that would allow me to secretly test the acoustics in each room. Call it a hobby.

"I hate the décor," he said with a huff. "I was dating a designer who insisted the nautical theme would be good either for resale or rental value. Never bothered me until I had to live with it day in and day out. Haven't gotten around to redoing it."

"What would you prefer?" I asked.

"That's the thing, I don't know. I used to be so modern, with boxy looks and sharp corners, but that style feels cold and stiff to me now."

Ten years was a long time to be indecisive. Then again, given the recent list of home improvements and upgrades I needed to make, I wasn't one to judge.

"I sold all my other houses," he said, answering an unasked question. "It's mostly just maintenance fees and property taxes here now."

"Same with me," I said. "Good that you kept this one, though. I mean, good choice. Good location, too."

"How come you never bought one out here?" he asked.

"I opted for practicality over paradise."

He took me into the final room on the main floor, a fantastic atrium-like space with a cathedral ceiling, furnished with a plump white sectional flanked by end tables, a glass coffee table, and tall, leafy plants that I couldn't discern as real or fake. And the focal point: a Steinway piano in the opposite corner, and floor-to-ceiling windows overlooking the majestic ocean and stretches of beach a half-mile out by a boardwalk leading from the back deck, with sand that practically massaged your bare feet. I may not have owned East End real estate, but I'd frequented the beaches here many times. Nothing else compared in greatness. And that was saying a lot, given how many beaches I'd been to all over the world.

My breath paused upon sight and sound of the waves crashing below, and I was engulfed with envy. *I should have bought a house here. I should have been less sensible and more nurturing.*

"How do you not live in this room?" I asked in almost a whisper.

Garrett sat at the piano. "Get this. The acoustics are great." He played the opening bars of ELO's "Can't Get it Out of My Head."

If there is heaven, it has to be a room with that piano and those acoustics, and an angel taking requests for eternity. And no "Piano Man."

Between the music and the view, I was close to swooning.

I especially had to keep myself from staring at Garrett. Not because I was starstruck—I'd gotten past that two minutes after meeting him when I was seventeen—but because he looked so…*average*. He looked as much like a pop star as I did these days. And yet, he was still oozing charisma, an aura of so many pop stars or actors that had nothing to do with facial features or body type or even talent. It pulled you in like a magnet, gave you goose bumps, made you wish you could bottle it.

He played a few more bars, and I caught myself hoping he would sing, but he stopped as abruptly as he started and stood up. "Fancy a drink of something?"

"Just water," I replied. Garrett excused himself, and I sat on a nearby sofa and gazed hypnotically out the window until he returned with two twelve-ounce, label-free glass bottles and handed one to me, cold to the touch.

"These days I don't drink anything stronger than herbal tea," he said with a self-deprecating chuckle. "God, if the kids could see us now…" He trailed off, then took a swig from his bottle. Somehow, I knew to whom he was referring when he said "kids"—our former selves, and the teenage fans who grew up with us. I wondered if "us" was he and myself or he and Gav and his Taro bandmates, or perhaps the whole lot of us. He reclined at the other end of the sofa, placing considerable distance between us.

"So how've you been?" he asked. As if we were old friends, catching up. As if this invitation was a reunion rather than whatever it was supposed to be. "What are you working on these days, besides our songs?"

There he was. The Garrett I'd been waiting to show up. Always with a snarky, passive-aggressive dig on hand.

I ignored it. "A record here and there," I said. "You?"

He scratched the top of his head. “Same,” he said, although I saw the truth behind it: *nothing.*

“Do you have a studio?” I asked. It occurred to me that I hadn’t seen one during the house tour.

“Upstairs,” he said. “One of the bedrooms. I don’t do much recording these days. I mean, I still play almost every day just to keep in shape, but no point in putting it on tape”—he corrected himself—“hard drive,” he said with the roll of his eyeballs.

“You miss it?”

He took another swig. “So, about those remixes…”

I straightened my posture. “Look, I didn’t intend—”

“I have to admit, they were brilliant. I was driving into town when Michael called me, told me to pull over immediately and listen to them. So I did just that and was highly impressed, and that was after one listen on the iPhone without earbuds. I raced home and played it on good speakers and was almost angry because it was how they should have sounded all along. I had no idea, Paisley.”

“Joey.”

“Sorry. Joey. Seriously, I had no idea you were still in the business. I thought you had fallen off the earth, too.”

Something about that hurt me—especially the *too.* Then again, that was Garrett—blunt. Unapologetic. Speaks before he thinks. I might have liked him more had he been like Gav, who had always spoken with intention rather than impulse. He used to take an extra moment to consider what he wanted to say and how he wanted to say it. He listened. He engaged.

Thing is, despite his delivery, Garrett was often right.

“Not really much business these days,” I said.

“You’re telling me.”

“I did the remixes for fun. I had some time off, got access to the tracks, and just started messing around.”

"That's what you do when you're bored? Shit, I'd love to hear what you do when you're under contract."

He already knew what I did under contract.

"I'm glad you liked them," I said. "I finished a fourth one on Saturday."

He put his fingers to his lips, as if a cigarette was attached. The gesture seemed involuntary; I'm not sure he even realized he'd done it. "Which one?"

"'Snowy Haze'."

"What did you do?"

"Replaced the drum loops with live drums. Softened them a bit to suit the ballad. Got rid of the woofy bass and added an acoustic guitar at the second verse. It's subtle, but it adds ambiance."

He nodded slowly, intrigued.

"Can I hear it? Did you bring it with you?"

I extracted my smartphone and earbuds from the knapsack I carried around in lieu of a purse. I scrolled until I found the track and handed it to him. He inserted the earbuds, closed his eyes, and listened, occasionally bobbing his head, and raised his eyebrows at what I assumed was the new guitar part. I inched to the edge of the seat, in anticipation and desire of his approval. He opened his eyes and said, "The drums are so much better. EQ is better, too."

"Thanks," I replied.

He listened a second time before removing the earbuds and handing the phone back to me. "What did you think of the album before you got your hands on the tracks?" he asked.

I took a pull from the water bottle before answering. "I got what you were trying to do. Or rather, what Timmy was trying to do."

"That makes one of us," he muttered.

"And the songs weren't bad. I just don't think they were well served."

"I was dragged into that album kicking and screaming. Was outvoted by the guys. They were itching to get back onto the charts, so they sold their souls. Working with Timmy was Warner's idea. Said he'd bring us into the twenty-first century. We couldn't get signed otherwise. Timmy was flummoxed the moment we walked into the studio with actual instruments. And he hadn't listened to our previous albums. Can you imagine that? What producer doesn't listen to your stuff? He only knew the hits. Said he didn't want what we'd done in the past to taint what we did in the present."

He backpedaled. "I mean, he's not a bad guy, and he's had a bunch of hits, so he's doing something right, but come on."

"The drum loops were awful," I said, gambling with a bit of Garrett's own bluntness. "Downright dull."

"Yeah, I'm probably to blame for that. I refused to bring in a real drummer. I'm sure you can understand why."

I nodded.

"But still," I said. "Michael's a good programmer. And you guys have done electronic music before. What happened?"

"Timmy vetoed us on everything. The least control we've ever had on an album. He played the you-don't-know-what-the-kids-are-listening-to-these-days card on us—which was complete bollocks, by the way—and threatened to go to Warner when we wanted to do things our way. And he said it would be fine on earbuds, which is the only way anyone listens to music anymore."

"That's what he lives for," I said. "The beats and the bass."

Garrett shook his head, as if the experience still baffled him. "This wasn't exactly a passion project for him. A one-and-done. When he and I got into a row, he took great pleasure in telling me that Warner had to beg him to work with us. And the others knew that without Timmy, we'd be right back where we started, which was nowhere. I told them we were better off nowhere. Or, at the very least, releasing it ourselves, but Benny was vehemently against the idea of Taro being an indie band. He's a bit of a snob that way."

"Ian had some good vocals. Just a little canned." Funny how in all the time I'd been a fan, I'd never once called Ian "Benny."

Garrett leaned an elbow back on the arm of the sofa and rested his head on his hand. "I don't know. Maybe we're a dying breed. Maybe sound quality and style really doesn't matter anymore. I never thought I'd feel out of place in this business, stuck in the past, wishing to go back to the way it used to be." His voice was wistful and distant.

"I know what you mean," I said.

"I didn't even want to promote the album," he said. "Didn't want my name on it. It was an embarrassment. Even the tour was a disaster. We did shows in the UK, that's it. Benny came down with laryngitis, and the rest of us took it as an omen. We cancelled what few gigs we'd already booked here in the States."

"I'm sorry."

He shrugged. "There was more to it, you know?" He gazed out the windows, somewhere beyond the ocean. "We'd never toured without Gav. Never did any of it without him."

I flashed back to my first Taro concert—the music practically drowned out by the roar of teenage girls in heat as Ian seductively thrust his hips. Garrett and Johnny, playing off each other before bouncing back to their mics. Michael, behind a fortress of synthesizers, animated and amorous.

And Gav. Beautiful. Devilish in grin, yet romantic at heart.

Rascally. He somehow managed to woo the crowd behind his kit. Would've kissed each girl there. And certainly every girl would have welcomed a kiss. Especially me.

"Your heart wasn't into it," I said.

"I don't think any of us knew how hard it was going to be. I mean, *I* knew, but..." he took a final gulp of water. "I relapsed after that album. That was the other reason why we cancelled the tour. I had to go back into rehab."

The weight of his confession—the *candor*—landed on me. It was stitched with shame, disappointment, grief.

"I didn't know," I said.

Garrett set the empty bottle on the end table and turned to me. All traces of sorrow vanished, as if all it took was the flick of a switch.

"So let's get down to it," he started. "Your remixes opened a vein with the band. They want to try one more time, go back into the studio and make an album, a good one this time. And they want you to produce it."

For a split second, I imagined how thirteen-year-old Joey would have reacted. She would've have let out a *squeeeeee*, would have danced around the room, would've called Laurel and screamed into the phone and afterward wrote *Dear Diary, you are NOT going to believe this...*

But adult Joey didn't even gasp. Because by the time I'd recorded my own demos and gotten a contract, I had decided to be Taro's peer rather than their fan. And yet, my insides swirled and stirred and whirled in a frenzy. Because some part of me had always known this moment could happen, *would* happen. Because I'd always wanted it to happen. Wanted it as badly as I'd wanted to be in the business. I just never thought it would have taken this long.

Been too long. How ironic.

But it was also too late. In every way.

"What about Jon?" I asked.

"Ravelle? We kind of burnt that bridge—rather, *I* kind of burnt that bridge," he replied. *What a surprise.* "He won't be working with us again. And Edgar's gone too, rest his soul. Took the magic with him, I'm afraid."

It's possible I missed Edgar Naturally almost as much as I missed Gav and Uncle Oscar.

"Yes, I knew about Edgar," I said. "Tremendous loss." After a beat I added, "So why don't you do it? Produce yourselves, I mean."

Garrett exhaled a drag of invisible smoke from that same imaginary cigarette as before, his head still resting on his hand. "That would pretty much be a disaster."

I pressed him. "You said the band wants to make another album. What do *you* want to do, Garrett?"

"I just don't see the point of doing it without Gav. It's too big a hole to fill. The Tin Man without his heart, or something."

"The Tin Man managed rather well for a long time without a heart," I reminded him.

"OK, so pick someone else," he snapped. "Thing is, I'd planned on a lifetime of making music, and at twenty-five years old my best years were behind me. Ian's had a pretty good run at cinema and telly roles, but I know he misses the stage and the music and the adulation from the crowds. He wasn't born for behind the curtain. And Johnny and Michael have done well as session guys and joining others on stage as guests. I just don't know what to do with myself. I never have. I miss being in a band, but I miss my brother more. They say that shit gets easier over time, but it doesn't."

He was right about that. For all the years that had passed since losing both Gav and Uncle Oscar, life had certainly gone on, as had my career. There was still plenty to be grateful for, and my love for the work never waned. But existential *happiness*? Without the two most important people to share it with, it had eluded me. Garrett and I were more alike in that regard than I had previously considered.

He continued, saying, "And I know you and I have had our differences in the past"—*an understatement*—"but I thought we could put them behind us."

I'd thought they *were* behind me. But sitting there with Garrett, I realized they had been nothing more than dormant. And maybe they needed to be dealt with once and for all. But was a recording studio the place to do it? I was, first and foremost and always, a professional. My job often required listening to the artists I worked with. Not their music—*them*. Their ideas. Their fears. Their hearts' desires. I had to be able to interpret and execute their vision, understand their personalities, speak their language. I would spend days, sometimes even weeks with them before beginning a project. Sometimes I needed to be a counselor, other times a referee. How could I do that objectively with Taro?

"I mean no disrespect to your relationship with Gav, but try to look at it strictly from a commercial point of view. Led Zeppelin moved on without John Bonham. The Who moved on without Keith Moon. I don't mean to say that Gav is so easily replaceable, but I think your fans, and future fans, would be OK with Taro doing the same. It's not forgetting him or discounting the monumental role he played. It's making something new. Something that could be just as good, albeit different." I paused for a beat before adding, "Something *he* would be proud of."

Garrett's attention went to the ocean again. I wasn't sure if he'd even heard me. At least one full minute passed before he spoke. "In hindsight, I'd wanted *Been Too Long* to fail from the start, and I sort of sabotaged it. I'd wanted to prove to them that we couldn't do it without Gav. Lately, I've been thinking about going back into the studio with the guys, trying again, but only with someone who knows what they're doing, and without the pressures of record company wahoos breathing down our necks. Make the music first, worry about getting it out there later. No label, no contract, and nothing to lose. The way we did in the very beginning, when it was new and exciting and fun. I can't remember the last time I had fun making music."

Wasn't that why I was getting out? Because making music had stopped being fun? It hadn't occurred to me that I worked my ass off not only because I desperately wanted to get every note right, but also because I desperately wanted to be accepted by my peers, to prove that a woman could be just as good a drummer and songwriter and producer and engineer as a man. It further occurred to me that maybe I'd been trying *too* hard, that all I really had to do was sit back and enjoy it.

Let's face it—I made music because I was a musician. I couldn't not do it.

Could I do one more album? Fulfill the one item still on the bucket list? Make Edgar and Gav and Uncle Oscar and Laurel proud one more time?

"There's no point in doing it if you don't want to, Garrett," I said. "You'll only end up with the same results as before."

"I know."

"Besides, do you really want *me*? I mean, do you think we can…" I trailed off. I just couldn't let myself go there.

Wherever Garrett had just gone in his mind, he exited his

reverie and returned his attention to me. "Did you really have fun doing those remixes?" he asked.

"I really did."

"Maybe we can officially release them as a special edition EP. Maybe it will get a little buzz going with the fans, give them something to look forward to when they find out we're back in the studio—*if* we go back into the studio, that is."

"Maybe," I said. "Maybe we just go straight into new material."

"That would be OK, too."

An ember smoldered within my solar plexus, threatening to be stoked.

I straightened in my seat again. "Garrett, I think Taro should go into the studio and make the best record it can. You should make the album *you* want—you and the band, including Gav. You think he won't be there, but he will. He's always been a part of you. He's a part of me, too. He's in every record I've ever worked on because I always thought about what he would do and how he would do it, and I imagined him sitting there, listening, approving."

He seemed touched by this revelation, yet his eyes went dark.

"Do *you* want to do it?" he asked.

The question caught me off guard, yet I knew the answer: *Hell, yes.*

I replied more reluctantly, however. "If Ian and Michael and Johnny are in, and you're in, then I'm in," I said.

But after everything that's happened, could I really be?

"Are *you* in?" I asked.

"I guess I owe it to the guys and the fans to try."

"You can't 'try,' Garrett. You need to *commit.* It's all or nothing."

He gazed beyond the window again.

"Do it for *him*," I added, my voice quavering. Garrett looked at me, his eyes glassy.

He took in a breath. "OK," he said on the exhale.

CHAPTER SEVEN

"I'm not a pop star and I never want to be a pop star! I wanted to be a musician all my life though, really."
~ Green Gartside, Scritti Politti

I remember reading those words in a magazine—although I can't remember which—when I was seventeen years old and empathizing with Green Gartside's point of view. And I loved Scritti Politti's album *Cupid & Psyche '85.*

Except I *was* a pop star.

It's not that I'd never wanted to be one—I loved popular music, loved its unapologetic got-a-good-beat-I-can-dance-to sensibility. Loved being able to sing simple lyrics that didn't have to reveal the meaning of life ("Silly Love Songs," anyone?) despite being moved to tears every time I listened to Brian Wilson's introspective "I Just Wasn't Made for These

Times." And the exhilaration of hearing my songs on the radio, watching them climb up the charts, was as intoxicating as being on stage. And that's what's addictive—the exhilaration and the adulation. Pop stardom is a surefire way to get it.

Gavin Chandler had signed up for all of it—he relished being a pop star, welcomed being plastered on bedroom walls and having teenage girls faint at the sight of him. He encouraged fan letters containing marriage proposals and was turned on when he would find a fan hiding in his hotel room closet or under the bed.

I had been one of those fans. Not that I ever hid in his closet, but I was among the hundreds of thousands of girls who wanted to be chosen by Gav, to be seen as more than a fan, to be *the* one.

Truthfully, I was in love with Gav for his musicianship more than anything else. In fact, that was the answer to "What Paisley Parker Wants For Christmas" in the *Rolling Stone* feature. *"I want bands like Taro to be seen as more than pretty faces,"* I'd told the journalist. *"I want people to see that behind the glare of stardom, there are serious musicians. Gavin Chandler is a world-class producer and songwriter, and that was before he hit 20. I get that it's hard to take any 20-year-old seriously, much less a teen star, but he deserves that consideration. And I want it for myself, too."*

When "Glossy" first came out, Laurel had been the only one to know the lyrics were about Gav.

Someday I'll fall through that glossy page
And see you face to face
My voice will be your song
To you my heart belongs
And you'll know. You'll know and love all of me for real

I sang that bridge with the intensity of wishing on a star or rubbing a genie's lamp. Hell, I might have sold my soul for its coming true. And maybe I had when I'd agreed to be Paisley Parker.

When I became famous, I met a lot of famous people. The original MTV VJs. Don Johnson and Phillip Michael Thomas. Daryl Hall and John Oates. I even met my two hero Carol(e)s—King and Kaye—and did a print ad for Simmons drums with Ringo Starr. (*Can you imagine that? Me and a freaking Beatle?*) There's always an adjustment that your eyes must make with each person, from two-dimensional print or TV screen size to three-dimensional life-size. Their voices sound slightly different in person than on TV. Their teeth aren't as white. They have a scent, infused with cigarette or pot smoke or alcohol or perfume or cologne or coffee. And then there's a little click in your brain that switches on and says, "Oh. Right. They're as human as I am."

The first time I met Taro was at the MTV Video Music Awards the year "Glossy" went to number one. The video was on constant rotation on the cable music channel. Backstage was a cacophony of celebrities and production crew members and makeup artists and a lot of booze, and we were all in a green room with press. Michelangelo might as well have chiseled Ian, Johnny, Michael, and Garrett and Gavin from marble, they were so beautifully sculpted. They were charming. Chatty. Drunk. Garrett, especially. Gavin Chandler was the glossy object of my dreams. When he and I were introduced for the first time, he was life size like the rest of us, but he was also larger than life. I fought every urge to be starstruck, resisted acting like every fan begging to go home with him and putting another notch on his belt of sex partners.

We didn't have much interaction that night—too much

chaos and mischief—but when we parted ways, Gav bid me "t'rah"—a British colloquialism for "'til we meet again" or "see ya"—and he held his dazzling gaze on me for just a few extra seconds—enough to make me think the moment was foreshadowing, that perhaps we would meet again. Not in another awards-show-after-party-who's-who kind of event, but something more intimate.

Within the next few years, Taro and I had more shared gigs. Promotional appearances. Press events. One-off performances with shared billing. The band members were witty and charming, as was I, and we got along easily. The most memorable had been the party to celebrate the legacy of Abbey Road Studios, which resulted in the photo of Gav and me that now sits at my mix desk in my own studio.

And with each parting of company, Gav bid me "t'rah."

Yet when my manager called me a few months after the Abbey Road event, the last thing I expected her to say was "Gavin Chandler will be in New York next week and would like to meet you at the Palladium."

"I would be happy to," I said with the professionalism of an executive. My double-time heartbeat and instant goose bumps, however, said something else.

Oh, how I could have used Laurel's fashion advice for that meeting. But Laurel was enrolled as a sophomore at the SUNY Binghamton. Besides, had I called and told her, she would have driven her beater Chevy Nova all the way from Binghamton to join me, and I selfishly didn't want that. No, I would tell her after the fact, make it sound as if Gav and I just so happened to run into each other at the Palladium.

I did hire a personal stylist at Bergdorf Goodman and found an outfit suitable for the occasion—dressy, but not prom-style. Trendy, but not who-are-you-wearing pretentious.

And when I arrived around eleven o'clock that night, I soaked in the widened eyes of recognition from the snake-like queue of patrons, and shouts of "Oh my God, it's Paisley Parker!" as the bouncers opened the doors for me. I found Gav in one of the VIP rooms, with a spread of hors d'oeuvres and champagne and fresh flowers set at a table.

Gav grinned widely when he saw me, his eyes flickering like flashbulbs, and he approached me with his hand extended. He had the longest lashes of any man I'd ever known; something about that made him even more magical.

"Paisley," he shouted above the dance music. "It's great to see you again."

His hand was like a hot towel. And yet it felt comforting, cleansing.

"You can call me Joey," I beamed. "Or Johanna. That's my real name."

"Even better," he said. "How was your Christmas?"

"Nice," I said. "Quiet. And yours?"

"Same." He then switched gears. "You know, I never thanked you for the kind things you said about me and Taro in that *Rolling Stone* article a few years ago. We can't get most thirty-year-olds to see what you saw in us, and it means a lot."

I could have melted into a puddle right there. But I retained my form and composure. "I'm flattered that you read it," I said. "And I meant every word."

"That's what made me want to get to know you. It also made me go listen to the rest of your stuff. I only knew 'Glossy,' of course—what a great song—and your other hits. You're one of us, Johanna."

You're one of us. I had never felt more validated in my life. Like the moment Pinocchio becomes an actual boy.

It took what felt like an eternity for me to speak, yet all I could muster was "I don't know what to say."

"We should work together," said Gav. "Maybe officially tour as a double-billing when our new album comes out."

"I would be honored. And I can't wait to hear the new album."

"I can play it for you in the car, if you'd like."

If I'd like!

"In fact, let's get out of here," he said, and with that we conspicuously left the club together, food and flowers untouched. I'm forever grateful we didn't live in the age of the Internet, when smartphone snapshots would have plastered social media in a matter of seconds. But back then, the report went no further than Page Six of the *Daily News* gossip column, and no more than a sentence or two.

In the limo, Gav played what would be Taro's fourth and final album with him, called *Major Arcana*, and of course it was brilliant. And unlike *Off Sides*—a deviation from their pop style but still musically brilliant, albeit commercially unsuccessful—*Major Arcana* would win back critics and produce one top-five hit, "Temperance." Yet as far as the rest of the world would be concerned, Taro was out the door with the eighties.

I had anticipated that Gav would make a move on me in the car, or instruct the limo driver to take us back to his hotel. And I wasn't sure how I would handle it. Fantasizing about having sex with Gavin Chandler was one thing—doing it was something else. Did I want to destroy that fantasy? Did I believe myself worthy? Or was I frightened that I would be nothing more than a one-night-stand to him? Instead, Gav suggested we go for a drive, and we just…talked.

We talked about our childhoods and coming of age on stage rather than in school. We talked about our overlapping musical influences, and I grilled him about what Jon Ravelle and Edgar

Naturally were really like. We talked about where we wanted to take our careers, and what we loved and hated about fame. Gav talked incessantly about Garrett, and what it was like to be a twin, while I opened up about the loneliness of being an only child whose parents never really understood her, and how Uncle Oscar and Aunt Mary Lou filled in those gaps.

We talked until three in the morning.

And during those hours, any traces of fangirl that might have still resided in me had dissolved. What's more, for the first time in years, I'd ceased to be Paisley. I was Johanna again. That's whom Gav wanted to talk to. As if he saw my whole person.

When the limo finally pulled up to my hotel (I'd opted to stay in the city rather than take the Long Island Rail Road home so late), Gav took my hand and kissed it.

"Johanna," he started. "I have to fly back to London tomorrow—or rather, in a few hours since it already is tomorrow," he said as he looked at his Swatch watch before taking my calloused fingertips into his hand again. "And then Taro is going back on the road next week to stir up excitement for the new album. We've not been to Italy or Australia or Japan for years. I would like to do so much more than kiss you, but to solicit more would be to ruin a perfect evening. And this evening was thoroughly perfect."

I was glued to his eyes. Tropical pools that contained universes in them.

"You're not a shag," he said. "You're someone I want to really know. And I want to know everything."

"I want to really know you, too," I said, my voice breathy, my body trembling.

He leaned in, and I closed my eyes as our lips met. I'd not kissed many boys in my life. And Gav was no longer a boy, nor I a girl. But that kiss was beyond any I'd ever experienced before. It was sensual. Sweet and bubbly, like champagne. It turned my heart into a balloon that floated beyond the confines of the car. And when we opened our eyes, I knew we both felt it, said it silently—the moment when life as you know it will never be the same.

We belong to each other.

"I wrote it for you," I said just above a whisper.

"Wrote what, love?" he asked, caressing my cheek with the back of his hand. His voice was the sound of vanilla glaze.

"'Glossy.' It was about you." I blushed the instant I confessed, and the car became a sauna. Gav glistened, his entire face a Christmas tree.

"Well," he said. "And now I know and will love all of you for real."

And that was it. There would never be another in my heart.

He winked, kissed me again, and said, "I am going to phone you when I am back in London, and we are going to make plans."

"Plans for what?" I asked.

"For forever," he replied. And with that he left the car.

I'd told Laurel none of this. Tried several times, but the words never came. It was as if nothing and no one belonged inside that bubble except Gav and me.

For the next four months, I worked in the studio while Taro toured. I practically skipped to the mailbox every day in anticipation of a letter or a postcard from Gav. With a copy of Taro's itinerary in hand, I, in turn, would send letters ahead to the next hotel they would be staying at. Additionally, we racked up hundreds of dollars in long distance phone calls, talking for up to two hours at a time. And every letter and phone call ended the same: "T'rah. I cannot wait until I am in your arms for the rest of our lives."

When I finally did confide in Laurel, she was surprisingly skeptical. "How can it be a real relationship when you're not in the same country, let alone the same room? I mean, you haven't even had sex yet."

Stung, I retorted, "In case you hadn't noticed, neither Taro nor I have easily compatible schedules. Pop stars rarely do."

I'd never played the I'm-famous-and-you're-not card with Laurel until that moment. She got the message.

The week of the Grammys—at none other than Radio City Music Hall—Taro flew to New York to be presenters.

Finally, Gav and I had a chance to be together in all the ways we'd been planning and dreaming about. We went for walks in Central Park. We drove out to the Hamptons for a day—he told me he and Garrett had made an offer on a house, sight unseen.

And yes, we did make love. Finally.

He wasn't my first, but he might as well have been. It was better than anything I'd ever fantasized about or experienced. Sex with Gav was as perfect as he was. As *we* were.

In fact, everything with Gav was better than anything I'd ever fantasized about.

"We'll get married when the tour is over," he'd said.

Making plans for forever.

"But my tour will begin," I replied.

"Then we'll squeeze it between the two, and I'll come on the road with you. Maybe I'll even join your band."

"Not even married yet and you're already kicking me off my kit?" I joked.

He kissed me jauntily. "My darling, we shall keep the beat together."

Then came That Final Night.

The night of the Grammys.

The night the light that was Gavin Chandler was snuffed out for good, when he stormed out the stage door and into the alley, retrieved the car he'd rented all week so we could get around freely—and tore out.

Drunk.

He lost control of the car, ran off the road, and smashed into a telephone pole.

Hence, our forever plans were as mangled as his car and body, pulled out with the Jaws of Life but dead on arrival.

The world grieved.

In the following days, I'd tried to telephone the band's management and leave a message for Ian, Michael, Johnny, and Garrett, and reached only a busy signal—that was normal in those days. I didn't have any of their personal numbers. In fact, I wasn't sure what or how much—or even if—the rest of the band knew about Gav and me, aside from Garrett, whose disapproval had eroded our happiness. Gav had told me that week that he was going to "talk to the guys" after the Grammys, when they'd have some time off. Given that none of them had reached out to me, I'd guessed that regardless of what they knew, it wasn't enough to matter to them.

I'd considered flying to England for the funeral, but I was afraid of being seen as an opportunist trying to get on an A-List. MTV News reported it as "a private family affair," with fewer than one hundred people. Not to mention that I suspected Garrett would make a scene of throwing me out if I showed up.

Two months later, a memorial concert was arranged, with proceeds going to a children's hospital charity that Taro supported. I vehemently pushed to get myself on *that* billing, however, and it turned out I didn't have to push at all—Michael Spaulding had already put me on the list of performers. Unlike other gigs, this time Taro were isolated from the other acts—they not only didn't perform but also didn't even show their tear-streaked faces until the very last guest—the Eurythmics—performed their set.

I could hardly get through my own three-song set, consisting of my hit "Too Good To Be True," The Beach Boys's "God Only Knows" (Gav's favorite song), and Taro's first single, "Crush." Every band/artist performed at least one Taro song.

My voice broke during every number. I opted not to play drums, not wanting or trusting myself to keep the beat on my own.

I tried to process my grief the only way I knew how—in the music. A few months after the memorial concert, I recorded a cover of Johnny Hates Jazz's "Shattered Dreams." I'd slowed it down to more of a piano ballad. Took me at least six takes before I could get through the vocals without bursting into tears. And although it charted, it didn't crack the Top 50. Reviews panned it as "too depressing." Clark Datchler called to compliment me, yet added: "Your grief was so raw. I can't listen to it and not weep. I think that's why it didn't sell."

Or maybe because it wasn't Paisley Parker singing it. It was *Johanna*, the one Gav knew.

I could have asked Clark how he knew I'd been grieving, but he's a musician. Just like Green Gartside.

My record label dropped me after that, and I became a full-time producer and engineer, opting out of the spotlight and into the control booth.

Uncle Oscar died of a heart attack a month later. He was the only person who'd fully supported Gav and me. Believed it was real, true love. Then again, he and Aunt Mary Lou had been the only ones who'd supported me in every way.

"There will be another," he had said to me during one of our final conversations, when I cried over Gav. "I know how broken your heart is right now, but don't hide your love away." I'd picked up on the Beatles lyric. He had a way of dropping such lines without cheapening the moment or the meaning behind them. "You're too much of a shining star. And I don't mean that in the fame sense. Gav saw that light, but he doesn't have to be the only one."

"He was my soulmate," I said. Gav knew it. I knew it. Even Uncle Oscar knew it.

"I refuse to believe you get only one," he said. "Especially if he dies young. That doesn't seem very merciful to me. And even if you do, that doesn't mean you can't ever fall in love again."

"How would I even know?"

"He'll tell you," Uncle Oscar said. And after a loving beat, he tacked on, "and so will I."

CHAPTER EIGHT

We all met at Janet St. James's office in Manhattan to discuss the new Taro album. It was the first time I'd seen Ian, Johnny, and Michael in more than twenty years. They had all aged, obviously, but more like a fine wine or a classic album as opposed to a Chevy station wagon. Now in their early to mid-fifties, their faces had long shed the formerly trendy, gender-bending makeup and were filled out with crow's feet and laugh lines. Ian's once-platinum, spiky hair was now straight, short, parted, and layered a salt-and-pepper ash brown, while the others still dyed their hair. The high-end couture gave way to functional jeans and Punk Masters graphic tees and button-down shirts, all still of designer quality.

We had all grown up, in more ways than one.

They were as amiable as always. Garrett, on the other hand, was all business.

I'd produced some big-name artists during my career. But even though they'd been out of the scene for so long, Taro was still undoubtedly the biggest in terms of fame and record sales and recognition. I wanted to impress them. I proposed a timetable and budget for the recording, production, and post-production costs, and they agreed with and accepted my estimates, which validated me.

"So who's putting up the cash for this little cotillion?" said Ian. "People don't buy music anymore. It's not like we can recoup our investment."

"I thought about that," I replied. "I propose you do a crowdfunding project and low-ball the figure. Say, forty percent of your budget. Ten bucks gets investors a CD or download. Twenty bucks gets them both the album and the remixed *Been Too Long*, signed by the band. Fifty bucks gets them the two albums—all formats—and a signed collector's poster. And so on."

Johnny picked up the thread. "And maybe kick in some swag, too. T-shirts. Key chains. Hats. Candid photos. Video updates."

"We could get that campaign up and running," Janet offered.

I nodded and continued. "Five hundred bucks gets them a video chat. A thousand bucks gets them an invitation to the launch party. I think your fans would love it. They haven't felt connected to you in such a long time, and I'm sure they miss you."

I thought about Laurel. She would be nodding vigorously.

"Brilliant," said Johnny and Michael, almost in unison. Even Garrett seemed agreeable. Janet St. James was on board as well.

Ian, however, disagreed. "What, we're a bloody charity case now? This is indie shit!"

"Would you get your head out of your ass, Benny?" Garrett retorted. It sounded like *O-S-S* rather than *A-R-S-E*. "Unless you want to pay for it yourself. In that case, have at it. But this is the way things are done now. And Joey has a point. We need to get our fans back, if we have any left."

"And whose fault is it if we don't?" barked Ian.

I interjected before Garrett had a chance to retort. "The fans are still there, and they will support you. It will probably make them feel like they're part of the project. They'll be proud. And ten bucks is what they'd pay for a digital download anyway."

"It's like they'd be buying the album up front," said Garrett. "Like a pre-order."

"Yes. Only instead of making a purchase, they're making an investment," I said. "It also ensures that they'd commit to an entire album and not just download one song. I know I'd send at least twenty bucks if I were a fan."

"You're not a fan anymore?" said Garrett with a smirk, his arms folded over his chest as he leaned back in his seat. Honest to God, I couldn't tell if he was teasing me or if he was genuinely disappointed.

I sat there, agape, when Michael chimed in. "And we could stay at Garrett's while we record. It would cut expenses."

Janet St. James chimed in: "We're absolutely in favor of that."

"So you're all going to squat at my flat, are you? Are you forgetting what happened the last time we lived in each other's pockets? We damn near killed each other."

"We were kids back then. Besides, what have you got, like, nine bedrooms in that house?" said Johnny. "Look, I think we all have to face the fact that we're starting over at square one. Kind of like our school days, when we were working odd jobs to pay for our guitars and bunking together in shitty hotels."

"Only now we're bunking at the beach," Michael said. "It could be worse."

Johnny persisted. "My point is that we're not recording in the south of France with personal chefs anymore. We have to cut some corners. And really, isn't that what made the challenge fun back then? I mean, yes, it sucks that at this stage of our careers this is what we need to do, but we've got the satisfaction of knowing we're working towards something."

"I'm happy to host you at my house, too," I added. "The view isn't as sweet, but...well, the offer stands."

Garrett waved me off. "No need. *Mi casa es su casa.* Unless you're bringing the wives and kids—then you're on your own."

"Our kids are grown up," said Ian. "Unlike some of us."

The quip elicited chuckles, but I had thought it was a little sharp. I had to learn these guys' temperaments. Their inside jokes. Their chemistry. As a producer, I was now entering their clubhouse. Some bands welcomed you there; others kept you at arm's length. You were, at best, more like a neighbor or acquaintance. But you were not the inner circle.

When I left Janet's office, I called Rick.

"How did your meeting with the dean go?" he asked.

I nervously tapped my fingers on the table at a Carl Palmer clip. "Yeah, about that..." I started. "How'd you like to come out of retirement and be lead engineer on an album?"

I could practically see and even hear his jaw drop. "Seriously?"

"Yes."

"*Your* album?"

"Taro's," I said.

He paused for a beat before replying, "You're kidding."

"I'm really not."

"The remixes?"

"Yep. They want to make a new album and tapped me to produce. I don't want to split duties, so I'm asking you to take over the desk. Mostly because you'll do it the way I want it," I said, which thankfully resulted in the laugh I'd aimed for.

"I thought you said there'd been some bad blood between you and one of the band members. Garrett, right?"

"Let's just say there's some water that hasn't quite gone under the bridge yet."

"Will it be a problem?"

"It won't interfere with my job, if that's what concerns you."

"It does," he said, "and those are famous last words."

"Rick, please. I really need someone I trust on this. I need the best. No joke. I need you."

"I need to think about it," he said.

He called me two hours later.

"Shit, Joey. You've got me."

"I know," I said with a laugh. "And thank you. Seriously."

On the first of April, Garrett Chandler, Ian Bensa, Johnny Rogers, and Michael Spaulding sat on the leather couch and a couple of swivel chairs in my studio.

Taro. In *my* recording studio.

It was just another gig, I told myself. But I knew better.

Unlike at the management meeting, here the conversations turned more casual, although we were still all business as we ironed out additional details.

"One other thing," I said. "On my watch and in my studio, there's no smoking, no drinking, and no drugs. If you show up tanked, trollied, hammered, wrecked, wasted, stonkered, snooted, juiced, baked, blitzed, lit, buzzed, maggoted, schnockmammered, or even just a little bit stoned, you're out."

"Blimey, you're no fun," said Ian. "I suppose you've found Jesus, too?"

"Last I heard, he's still following the Grateful Dead," I said.

Michael laughed as he turned to Ian and said, "I like this one," thumbing in my direction. Ian drew a tight hand to his forehead in salute, tilted his chin, and I knew at that moment that I earned his trust and respect.

I caught Garrett glancing at the drum kit in the corner and crinkling his eyebrows in puzzlement. "Something is..." he started. Then, it registered. He turned to me. "You're left-handed?"

I nodded. "You didn't know?"

"I guess I forgot." His attention then went to my Gibson acoustic in the opposite corner, the pick guard on the left side, and the custom left-handed Les Paul beside it, before returning to me. "A female producer, engineer, *and* left-handed. You really are a rare breed."

Resisting the distraction, I stayed on point. "I want to make a kick-ass album with you guys. I want to make the album we Taro fans all clamored for after *Fortune Tellers* but never got. I'm not talking about making *Fortune Tellers Two.* I'm talking about making an album that captures the *feeling* we got when we listened to *Fortune Tellers.* That tactile sense of holding an album in your hands, shiny and new, smelling the vinyl, spinning it on your turntable for the first time, and then letting the music meet you where you live. That sublime moment of being swept away—let's make that happen even on a smartphone."

"Wow, are you a romantic," said Garrett. "No wonder you

loved my brother. I guess you really did kiss his glossy every night." He laughed mockingly.

I fumed as if smoke were emanating from my ears.

Gav had to have told his twin brother my confession about "Glossy." Had to have trusted Garrett to keep the secret.

But I was *not* going to let Garrett Chandler go there.

I stood up and glared at him. "Come with me." I then pointed toward the control booth. To the others, I said, "Gentlemen, excuse us."

Garrett folded his arms and remained seated, wearing a smirk that I wanted to smack off his face. "Am I in trouble already?"

I moved in, towering close enough for him to lean back in his chair, and stared him down. He smelled like cinnamon and hazelnut, and, thanks to that and the vanilla candle I lit at the start of the meeting, I could've licked his cheek, the scent was so delectable. But I was too focused.

"You think you're the first asshole to treat me like this? Like I'm still Paisley Parker, pudgy pop star, with the cute little outfits? You think you're going to sabotage this project like you did the last one? Because we'll do it without you. Or maybe I won't do it at all. I'm not the one flat-lining here."

I regretted the choice of metaphor the instant it spilled out. I wanted to apologize, but instead I pressed on because I knew I needed to make the power play.

I also knew I wouldn't have had to were I a man.

"But this is my house, Garrett. *My* house. And I demand you treat me and your fellow bandmates with respect, because they, too, are guests in *my* house. And by the way, I've got more Grammys and gold records than you, so remember that the next time you mouth off to me about my romantic idealism. I am not Timmy Tonka, and I am not your groupie.

You are either on board with this album or you're not. And if you're not, then you can leave now."

Garrett glared at me, stone-faced.

With my peripheral vision I spied the others looking at their shoes like kids who'd just witnessed their teammate being rebuked by their soccer coach, not daring to speak or make eye contact.

"I'm going to take a few minutes," I said. "When I come back, you'll let me know if we're going to work together."

I exited the studio through the door leading up the stairs and into the house, trembling. From there, I made a beeline for the bathroom and forced myself not to let the tears escape from their ducts. *Don't be a girl, don't be a girl, don't be a girl...*

After splashing a couple of handfuls of cold water on my face, I took a deep breath and checked my reflection for traces of emotion. Adjusted my ponytail. Applied some Chap Stick to my lips. For the meeting at Janet St. James's office, I'd worn my hair down, applied makeup, dressed in black denim with a houndstooth sports jacket. Today I was in my usual studio attire of blue jeans and Sketchers and plain V-neck T-shirt.

Two more breaths, and I left the bathroom. As I descended the stairs to the studio, I could hear the guys shouting at one another.

"This is *my* band," yelled Garrett. "I'll fucking sue you if you try to make this album without me and still call it Taro."

"Get off it," yelled Ian. "We're done with the dictatorship. It's democracy or nothing. Look, mate, we had something everybody dreams of, and I fucking want it back. You weren't like this before. You really think you'd be acting this way if he were here? You think he'd *like* you like this?"

I inhaled and exhaled one more conscious, calming breath,

and cool, collected Joey returned. When I opened the door, the shouting halted.

"Let's not go there," I said. And then: "Garrett, may I speak to you privately in the control booth, please?"

Already standing, he acquiesced and followed me, probably because he was tired of one-against-three and was ready try his odds at one-against-one. I closed the door and leaned back against the desk. "I'm sorry for speaking to you like that in front of your peers. I'm especially sorry about the flat-lining comment. I needed to set a boundary."

He folded his arms again, mouth clamped shut, like a petulant middle school student.

"What's going on?" I asked.

He paused, staring beyond the walls, no doubt at a memory. "It was your drums."

"What about them?"

"You're left-handed," he said, as if the point was obvious.

And then I knew: *Gav was left-handed, too.* Had his kit arranged the same as mine—backward from the traditional set-up. They were the same drums I'd used in the mid-'80s, save a few upgrades. And the same brand—Ludwig—that Gav had used. I'd emulated him in that sense.

"I'm sorry," I said. "I should have been more conscientious." In fact, it was my job to be.

"You don't know what the triggers are, or when. Shit, *I* don't even know. They just ambush me from out of nowhere sometimes."

I flashed back to Gav on stage, his face aglow and not just from sweat, having the time of his life. He had perfect timing.

I then fixed my attention back to Garrett. "I really do want to make this album with you guys. As a fan, as a musician, and as a producer. And it would be great to be a kid again, wouldn't it?" After a beat, I added, "Minus the acne and teenage angst."

A chortle escaped him, which was a win as far as I was concerned.

I stepped toward him, and this time my height betrayed me as my head reached his chin. I craned my neck to meet his eyes. "We're going to make your brother proud, I promise. I would never let you do anything less. And he's going to be right here with us."

"That's exactly what terrifies me," he said. "Why do you think I've avoided all this? Because I *don't* want him here. I *don't* want to be reminded of him. Because then I'll want *all* of him here. I'll want to *see* him. I'll want to *talk* to him and wrestle him like we used to when we were kids, and I won't be able to, and he'll die all over again and I swear I'll die right along with him this time. *I can't.*"

His voice broke on the last word, and a tear etched a path along the contour of his cheekbone. Suddenly, I ached for Gav in the very same way—his flesh and blood, his voice and laugh, his kiss and touch.

In any other situation, without our history, I would've hugged Garrett in consolation. Instead, I swallowed down the desire to do so, along with my ache.

I pointed at the control booth window. Johnny, Ian, and Michael were on the other side of it, talking and looking worried. "They're your brothers, too, you know. Don't you think they'll have your back? They always did. They still do."

He didn't respond.

"We want you, Garrett. We *need* you. But we need all of you. We need you to be fully present."

"I honestly don't know if I can be," he said, his voice soft, distant.

"Please?" I beckoned. I wasn't entirely sure I was speaking solely as a producer with a professional interest.

He perused the framed gold records along the back wall before he returned his attention to me and broke into a sly, sexy smile reminiscent of the "Raindance" video, the one that had always been my favorite. The mini-movie was an explosion of color—all five guys on a white bandstand with a white runway against a paint-splattered backdrop, costumed in white trousers and matching boots and each wearing orange and yellow and red T-shirts with bandanas, kicking, slashing, and stomping in puddles and splashes of dyed water, colors matching their shirts.

Not to mention they all looked sexy as hell when wet. Garrett and his twin brother had been practically indistinguishable in that video.

And with that smile, Garrett was still as sexy today.

Yet my heart felt as if it were constricting—was the discomfort because Garrett had caused it, or was I wishing Gav was the one standing in front of me sporting that identical smile?

"It would be nice to be a kid again," I said.

And as if he were reliving that very video moment, Garrett resolutely declared, "Yes, it would."

I could swear the room literally brightened. And then, unable to contain my goofy, so-not-sexy grin, I said, "Then let's go make a record."

CHAPTER NINE

After a lunch in my kitchen consisting of a submarine hero, chips, soft drinks, and cookies all from a local deli, Taro and I reconvened to the studio, ironed out last-minute details, and ended our meeting. I ushered the guys out the private entrance, one by one, when Michael asked to stay behind. "I want to check out the toys," he said of my instruments and gear.

I followed him back into the studio and was about to start with the keyboards when he interrupted me. "I'm sorry for the ruse, but I wanted to talk to you without the others."

Of the five Taro members, none had been cuter than Michael Spaulding back in the day. His spiky, jet-black hair tapering into a mullet (back when mullets weren't as...well, mullet-y) and ending halfway down his neck, loop earring, and inky irises; he had been brooding, a teddy bear you wanted to take home and cuddle. He was the shyest of the five, happy to be hidden behind racks of synthesizers, a team player rather than a leader. He'd also come to the band with more academic musical training than the rest of them, having taken classical piano lessons from age four to eighteen, even after Taro hit the top of the charts. He understood musical theory as it related and applied to composition.

These days, his hair color had softened to a sandy brown. Eyes were still inky, sunken into high cheekbones and framed by crow's feet. His lips, no longer pink and supple, were more like a dry neutral. He looked weathered, but he also looked optimistic. Youthful.

"We want this to work, and we're worried about Garrett making it hell for us. One minute he's calm and in control—sometimes literally—and the next minute he's abusive. I'm not unsympathetic to his grief, but he's been…well, he wasn't always like this. At least not before all the drink and drugs. He's clean now, and that's good, but he's still angry."

"I noticed that," I said.

"Johnny and Benny and I knew we were joining Gavin and Garrett's band. Garrett was the brain, and Gav was the heart. They never lorded it over us—we all had a say, and we just naturally deferred to them because we trusted them. We were kids. Like, *children*."

I instinctively knew where Michael was going, and picked up the thread. "But they were mature for their age," I said. "Visionaries, really."

"Absolutely," he replied. "They were smart and intuitive, and they were disciplined go-getters. They had a clear picture of where they wanted the band to go and how to get there. Plus, they had that twin thing going where I swear they really did have telepathy. We got our manager, our contracts, even our sound all because of them."

I nodded as I recalled my thirteen-year-old-self poring over every article, every interview, everything ever written or spoken about Taro. "Minds and talent like that are once in a generation. And when you have *two* of them synchronized like that…" I trailed off.

Michael turned sad. "Gav's death devastated all of us. He was a brother to me. We'd been certain that we were going to last for twenty, thirty, even forty years. Call that foolish thinking, but hey, look at the Stones. Look at McCartney. We believed in that kind of fortitude."

"You were on top of the world," I said. "How could you not believe that? Plus, you wouldn't have been wrong."

"None of us knew what to do after the accident, because none of us had wanted to do anything but be pop stars in a band. We've been wandering aimlessly ever since. Johnny, Benny, and I wanted to find a way to go on as Taro. But Garrett…he just couldn't. Taro without Gav was bad enough, but without Garrett? We knew the fans would never accept it, and we knew we couldn't be Taro musically without both of them. Part of me wishes we had tried harder, though."

"It's hard to start over, to reinvent yourself," I replied. "A lot of people thought Paisley Parker was a fraud, something the record company contrived. And they weren't entirely wrong about that. However, when I tried to be Johanna—same music, same sound—they hated the authenticity even more. Nobody wanted me to be me."

"It was my idea to have you produce," said Michael, and I was taken aback. For some reason I'd just assumed that the decision had been made collectively, or by the management. I'd never considered that one of them had specifically gone to bat for me.

"I think we could use a woman's touch, Joey," he said, and

instantly backpedaled. "No, strike that. We need *your* touch. You know us. You know our sound. You have great instincts. I've listened to just about everything you've ever worked on."

"Really?" I asked, simultaneously surprised and flattered.

"Yes," he said. "And I know you'll do right by us. I've never seen anyone besides Ravelle call Garrett out on his shit the way you did today, and believe me, it needed to happen. I think if anyone can bring out the best in our Garrett, you can."

Rather than feeling encouraged, I closed my eyes as my stomach churned. That was quite a gauntlet he'd just thrown down.

"Listen," I started. "Since you've been forthcoming with me, I should reciprocate. You should know that there's some history between Garrett and me."

Michael raised his eyebrows.

"Not *that* kind of history," I said. "At least not with him. I…I was supposed to be with Gav and…well, let's just say Garrett didn't approve." My body trembled as tears pushed to the gate yet again.

Michael stood momentarily frozen. "Joey, I had no idea. I mean, I remember you and Gav being friendly back in the day, but…"

I tried to picture seeing Gav and me from Michael's twenty-two-year-old point of view. Had he not noticed the way our eyes sparkled in each other's presence, how Gav touched my arm like the brush of a feather, accompanied by a warm smile? Could he not see the fireworks that emanated from me every time Gav entered a room I was in? Had Michael or anyone else not noticed the way Gav and I sometimes conversed in rhythm and harmony? Had I simply assumed it was obvious because it had felt so loud to me?

And then, Michael's eyes widened as he gasped. "Oh God,

was that *you*? I remember being on tour and Gav constantly talking about 'the one, the one.' We thought it was bollocks, like a passing fancy. Or that he was just drunk and in some kind of puppy love. But he was serious, wasn't he?"

I nodded as emotion welled in my chest. My eyes stung.

"Why didn't he come out and say it was you?" Michael asked.

I shrugged. "He had told me that he wanted to wait until the tour was over. Said he was going to tell you all after the Grammys."

Michael put a hand to his forehead, absorbing the shock.

"Christ, Joey. I'm so sorry. You lost him, too."

I blotted a tear from my cheek with the knuckle of my pointer finger. "We all did."

"But you *lost* him like we did."

It suddenly occurred to me that I'd lost even more than Gav. I'd lost *Taro*. The pedestal I'd placed the entire band on during my early adolescence was meant to be crumbled, but I had never noticed that the smashed and shattered pieces had crushed and buried me under the rubble. It was why, like Garrett, I was both scared and desperate to make this album. Not to rebuild the pedestal, but to finally dig myself out from under the collapse. Johnny, Ian, and Michael all had shovels. So did Garrett. But was he using it to dig a new hole?

I speculated as much to Michael.

"Garrett's never been easy to work with. None of us are. We fight like schoolboys when we're in the studio. You should know that up front. We just want to get it right. But we've always had chemistry musically, and a long time ago we were all close. Ian talks the most about wanting to be back on top, but I also know he most wants us to be close again."

"It's never going to be like it was before," I said. "It can't be." I was talking to me as much as to him.

"We don't want *before*," said Michael. "We want something new, but something…I don't know. Not quite nostalgic, but not quite retro. Repurposed, I guess. And not just musically. You get it, I know you do."

I did. But could I deliver?

He smiled, revealing traces of the boyish face he still had. "I'm really looking forward to working with you, Joey. I think we're going to be great mates when this is all over. Bloody shame we didn't do this thirty years ago. We might not be having this conversation now if we had."

Over my dead body, I remembered Garrett saying. And there was already one dead body too many. A death that was greater than the sum of the living bodies it left behind.

I strained under the weight of what we were all taking on. Michael, Ian, and Johnny—they all needed this to regain a sense of purpose in their lives. Garrett even more than the others. As if this album was one final brass ring for the taking. Had they been anything without Taro? John, Paul, George, and Ringo—they'd all found identities outside of the Beatles. But what if they'd still been together when Lennon was murdered? Would they have still been the Beatles without him? Would they have been able to continue?

What if there wasn't supposed to be a Johnny, Michael, or Ian outside of Taro? In other words, if the album failed—if *I* failed—what would happen to them? Would I be responsible for their ultimate demise?

I was pretty sure Garrett believed I already was.

And what about what was at stake for *me*? If this album succeeded, would I change my mind and continue my career, or should I still hang it all up, like I was planning to do?

If it failed, I wouldn't really have a choice in the matter. I would be done.

And let's face it: I really didn't want to teach.

When it came to aimless wandering, there was too much ground to cover.

"I'm going to make this work," I said. "For all of us."

Michael thanked me and shook my hand. "Now, let's see the toys. For real."

CHAPTER TEN

For the next two weeks I listened to everything I could get my hands on that was connected to Taro, Jon Ravelle, and Edgar Naturally. As far as I was concerned, *Fortune Tellers* was my generation's *Pet Sounds*—if not in sound and songwriting innovation, then certainly as a cultural and musical marvel. Aside from the fact that Taro was among the first bands to use sampling, not to mention layering electronic Linn and Simmons drums on top of live drums, their musical and lyrical themes were timeless. They wrote about where they came from. About family. About finding *the one*. They wrote about being at home inside of their own skin. They wrote about nuclear war without actually writing about nuclear war. They wrote about status quo and nonconformity. And they did it all to a danceable beat. If they hadn't been so young, so damn good-looking, so pinup perfect, and such MTV darlings, then I'm sure more of their fans' older siblings and even parents would have liked them, too. And yet, they loved being the object of so many screaming girls' affection. They fully embraced the look—the clothes and hairstyles and campiness of it all. They were teen trendsetters without even trying to be.

Jon and Edgar had a lot to do with actualizing that musical vision, thanks to their production and engineering expertise, but Gav and Garrett had had the vision in the first place. They all did, really. All of them could play—not just the three chords they'd learned from listening to the Clash or the Ramones but complex melodies from more *avant garde* influences like David Bowie and Roxy Music and Joy Division. They also knew slick production thanks to Jeff Lynne and Trevor Horn yet still maintained the mainstream pop sound of bands like Culture Club and Spandau Ballet. They weren't just riding the wave—they *were* the wave. Ahead of their time.

Back then, the critics hadn't given *Fortune Tellers* or Taro the credit they deserved because of their age and a lack of longevity. Some dismissed the album without even listening to it, writing Taro off as some contrived, Menudo-type band that only had to sing and look pretty while a team of marketers and stylists did the rest. Both Taro and I had been underrated, dismissed as teeny-bop pop, ignored for our contributions to songwriting and sound and production quality of albums being made by twenty- and even thirty-somethings during the same decade. Furthermore, no one listened to me when, at sixteen, I told a journalist who asked me about my favorite album: "Mark my words, we'll be talking about *Fortune Tellers* thirty years from now, and it will still sound fresh."

Sure enough, thirty years later *Fortune Tellers* made the top ten of every Best Albums of the Eighties list, as well charting favorably on the All-Time Best Pop Albums lists. My album *Next Wave* made some of those lists too, I'm proud to say.

Made me wonder how good Taro would have been had they continued. Also made me wonder if I would have been commercially better off had I remained Paisley Parker. A *thin* Paisley Parker, that is. The Paisley Parker the decision-makers at Capitol Records had wanted me to be.

I also took out some of my other favorite albums from that time: INXS's *Kick*, ABC's *The Lexicon of Love*, XTC's *Skylarking*, Cyndi Lauper's *She's So Unusual*, and Daryl Hall & John Oates's *Private Eyes*, plus some newer stuff from Kelly Clarkson and Mark Ronson and, for fun, *The Best of Burt Bacharach*. We were all in agreement about what we wanted this Taro album to be: original, yet commercially viable. Signature style—pristine production, upbeat pop songs as well as pensive ballads, something that not only didn't take itself too seriously but also wasn't too superficial. They wanted the sound to be retro but not dated. They wanted to use digital technology the same way cosmetics were used: to enhance the features already present, but not as replacements for aesthetics, not to mention talent. They also wanted to use as many live instruments as possible. In other words, *no drum loops*.

Which left us in need of a drummer.

And there was only one person I wanted, whom I believed could do Taro, and Gav, justice.

I called Garrett the day before the sessions were to officially begin.

"How would you feel about me being the drummer for this album?" I asked.

For a moment I thought the call dropped.

"Garrett?"

"Yes, I'm here," he replied.

"We agreed that we don't want to repeat the mistakes of *Been Too Long.* Michael could successfully program the drum tracks, but I think you know Taro needs a drummer. I also know that none of you want to bring just anyone into the fold. Neither do I."

More silence. I awkwardly rambled on. "I know Gav's style. Heck, I stole from him all the time. Still do."

I shut up and waited for him to speak.

Finally, he did. "I think you should audition."

I did a double take as if he were standing in front of me.

"Seriously?"

"Yes. When was the last time you played in a band?"

Of course, I still occasionally played drums during a recording session, still practiced regularly just to keep my chops up. But more often than not I was drawing on a digital database of synthesized sounds and samples and manipulating them at the mix board.

Playing live? With a band? For an entire album?

It had been a while.

Too long.

My silence answered the question.

"I thought so," said Garrett. "I want to see just how rusty you are."

I didn't think he'd say *Of course, terrific!* Not even *Sure, why not.* But I also didn't think he'd make me prove myself. Was this a power play on Garrett's part, exactly what Michael tried to warn me about? Or was I being defensive, and Johnny and Ian and Michael would also demand an audition from me? And perhaps they were even well within their rights.

Maybe this was just Garrett being afraid. Gav was irreplaceable, after all.

Or maybe he was more afraid that Gav wasn't.

"OK," I said. "Tomorrow we'll jam. I'll play whatever you guys want."

"Fine," he replied. "I'll let the others know. See you tomorrow."

After we hung up, I dialed Laurel next. She answered on the second ring, and I could hear a flurry of teenage voices.

"Hey, Laurel. Is this a bad time?"

"I'm taking Lila and her friends to soccer practice. Hope you don't mind being on speakerphone."

A chorus of hellos and who-is-that-mom hit my ears, followed by Laurel's shushing and a response of "It's your Aunt Jo-Jo." I appreciated that she wanted me to have a special relationship with her kids. I also felt guilty for not living up to it lately.

"I can call back later," I offered.

"I've got dinner and homework and a ton of other stuff to tend to tonight, so it might as well be now. What's up?"

"Well, I wanted you to know before the press release comes out: Taro is making a new album, and I'm going to be the producer."

She screamed. A full-throated, teen-girl scream. The tinniness of the shriek pricked my eardrum as I pulled away from the phone.

"Shit, Laurel!" I was about to apologize for cursing in front of the kids when I realized none of them heard it because they were screaming and laughing like the fifteen-year-olds they were. The way *we* once were, come to think of it.

"Oh my God! OH MY GOD, JOEY!" Before I could answer, she said, "And you were mad I put those songs on YouTube. YOU'RE WELCOME."

I had to admit it. She was responsible for getting me this gig. "Mea culpa," I said.

"Does this mean you're going to London?"

We arrived at the part of the conversation I was dreading. "Actually, they're recording here. At my studio."

This time I held the phone away in advance. Another scream.

"OH MY GOD, JOEY!"

"Listen, Laurel—"

"When do I meet them?"

I sucked in a breath.

"That's one of the reasons I'm calling you." I said. "This is business."

"What do you mean, it's business?"

"I mean, I can't just bring you over to the studio and introduce you like some groupie. We're going to be working."

"That's ridiculous," she said, the hurt hanging off the jagged edges of her words.

"Look, would your boss be OK with you bringing someone you know to meet them and watch them work? Because that's kind of what this is."

"It's not the same and you know it." Forget hurt. She was angry now. "God, Joey, this is so typical *you.* You can't stand to share."

"What?"

"That's why you never invited me to that big gala in the eighties."

"Laurel, are we seriously going to rehash this again? You know I was limited with how many people I could invite. It was more appropriate to bring my aunt and uncle. They did everything for me."

"But I'm your *best friend.* Or at least I'm supposed to be. You never wanted me to meet Taro because you wanted them all to yourself. Especially Gav."

"Who's being ridiculous now, Laurel?"

The car had gone awkwardly quiet, the girls aware that the adults were fighting.

"Tell me you weren't afraid Gav was going to fall for me instead of you. Or that Ian was. Or any of them. You didn't just want Gav for yourself. You wanted each and every one of them for yourself. You've always been threatened by me."

You could see it in photos of Laurel and me in junior high and high school before I became famous: She was the prettier one. The thinner one. The one all the boys liked and asked out. The one who got roses from secret admirers on Valentine's Day and was voted queen of the dance or the prom or whatever school event was going on.

And I had hopelessly envied her for it.

Laurel had supervised almost all my outfits back then. She had selected me the paisley scarf that gave way to my name. She taught me how to wear my hair and makeup. All I knew how to do was mic a drum kit. And it turned out that Laurel's skills were more useful than mine when it came to getting signed to a record label.

Socially, Laurel had poise and confidence. I had a great vocal range. The former beat out the latter at parties every time.

Even after I became famous, I knew the attention wasn't for *me*. It was for Paisley. But Laurel was a star without needing to practice an instrument for hours on end, or listen to records all day, or work a part-time job to pay for studio time.

Laurel was the main attraction simply for being Laurel. And most enviable of all, she didn't have to change her name.

All these years later, she was still a knockout. She still turned heads. She was creative and crafty and jaunty and generous.

For the first time ever, I confronted the ugly truth: *Maybe she's right.* Maybe that was the reason I'd not invited her to meet Taro all those years ago. Why I didn't want to introduce her now. After all these years, I still envied her. Still felt threatened.

I wanted to say *I'm sorry.* But instead I blurted, "You're wrong."

"I'm really not," she retorted.

I let out an exasperated sigh. "Fine. I'll see what I can do."

"Forget it," she said. "Don't do me any favors. I certainly won't be doing any more for you."

"Laurel," I started, and before I could say anything else, she hung up on me.

Well, shit. That didn't go well.

CHAPTER ELEVEN

I was a pots-and-pans kid.

Whereas Laurel used them, along with wooden spoons, for cooking and baking—she'd wanted to be a home economics teacher when she grew up, she said in the fourth grade—I used them for drumming.

My parents, of course, were not happy about this. They'd bought me Barbie dolls and Lite Brite and coloring books for Christmases and my birthdays, hoping I'd settle into a more quiet pastime, but hand me two sticks, two spoons, two pencils, and I'd eventually wind up tapping on tables and desks and car seats. I wasn't interested only in the rhythms but also in what kinds of sounds I could make. A sofa cushion made a muffled sound (good for a kick drum), while the bottom of a skillet was closer to a snare.

When I was eight years old, Uncle Oscar picked me up

after school and took me to the music shop a few doors down from his sporting-goods store. A guy with long hair and tie-dyed T-shirts named Dave Angelique taught me some basic counts and rhythms and time changes on a practice drum pad. I smuggled it home with a pair of drumsticks in my school bag, and because the pad was rubberized, I could practice in silence without my parents' knowledge. They exhaled, thinking their daughter's silly phase was over.

That is, until we went to Uncle Oscar and Uunt Mary Lou's for Christmas in 1981 and Santa Claus just so happened to have delivered a full drum kit for me there. Set up left-handed.

I could hear the shouting despite my banging out a year's worth of practicing and tutelage.

"There's no way that thing is coming into my house," said Dad.

"She's naturally talented, Robert," said Uncle Oscar. "You need to nurture that, not quash it."

"My daughter is *not* going to be a *musician*." He'd said *musician* with utter contempt. Less than. "Especially a *drummer*. She's a *girl*, for Christ's sake."

"A girl you all but ignore," said Uncle Oscar.

Remember that song Mr. Rogers used to sing on his PBS show *Mr. Rogers' Neighborhood*? It was called "What Do You Do With the Mad that You Feel."

I drummed.

My parents didn't speak to Uncle Oscar for months after that. They refused to let him pick me up after school anymore, either. So I rode my new bicycle—a gift from my parents that same year (they'd emphasized that Santa had nothing to do with it, that it arrived thanks to their hard-earned paychecks, Mom as an English teacher and Dad as an electrical engineer)—to and from school from then on, and to Uncle Oscar's whenever I could to practice. I moved from drum lessons to guitar and piano lessons at the music shop. Also taught by Dave Angelique. Aunt Mary Lou bought an acoustic guitar at a neighbor's garage sale, and Dave strung it upside down for me. I snuck out of recess to play the piano in the school auditorium.

I drummed in every school band—marching, brass, and even jazz—and sang in the shower. It was a passion, but it was also still just a hobby. I wasn't officially writing my own songs yet (that wouldn't happen until I heard Taro's first album), but I taught myself to play those of others by ear. My parents had—pardon the expression—drummed into me that musicians didn't make money, and that only guys were rock stars. Girls were singers like Donna Summer or Tina Turner or Diana Ross. Or they were backup singers, whose job was to "stand there and look pretty," as my dad had once said. Carole King was a songwriter, not a showman, I was told. ("And what's wrong with *that*?" I wondered.) Girl drummers were lesbians, and you'd think being a lesbian was worse than being a drummer, to hear Mom and Dad say the word with as much condemnation as the word *musician.*

Uncle Oscar debunked those notions at every turn. He told me about Carol Kaye, the bass player on Brian Wilson's *Pet Sounds* and the unfinished *Smile* album, and countless other recording sessions. I wouldn't see pictures of her until the age of the Internet. And it turned out Carole King *was* a leading act—she played piano and sang and was musically savvy in every way. Uncle Oscar played all those albums for me, taught me how to listen to them, what to listen for. He'd take me out for ice cream, name a Beatles song, and challenge me to identify the key by singing the first note. Or he'd sing the first bar, and I'd sing the harmony—he was especially impressed by my ability to harmonize. Neither he nor Dave had taught me that.

"They don't get me," I'd sobbed to Uncle Oscar one afternoon as he took me home, my bicycle crunched in the trunk of his Oldsmobile. I didn't want to go into the house. "Why did they have me if they didn't want me?"

"Listen, Joey. One day you'll be old enough to walk away. But you need to do what *you* want to do in life. Don't let anyone—even me—tell you what you should or shouldn't do or be. If you want to be a drummer or a singer or a songwriter, then do it. If you want to be an accountant, then do it. If you want to take over my store one day, then I'll help you do that. You don't have to do anything you don't want to do."

But I knew: I was going to be a professional musician. I was going to write songs. I was going to record them in a studio, and someday I was even going to produce them. I was going to go on the road and perform.

And, like Taro, I was going to do it before my twenty-first birthday.

I booked every gig I could, from birthday parties to twenty-minute sets at the Howard Johnson's lounge to the school talent show. I recruited two boys from gym class—Andy Lancaster on guitar and Evan Blue on bass—to form my first band called The Tiger Beats. It was short-lived; the guys wanted to play Bon Jovi and Def Leppard, and I wanted to play Taro as well as my own songs.

I got an after-school job answering phones in a recording studio, and thus received a twenty percent discount to rent it for my own recording. On the weekends I helped Uncle Oscar in his store, and in lieu of a salary, he covered the rest of my studio expenses and got me whatever equipment I needed. Still, we could afford to rent it only twice a month. The engineer, a guy named Tommy, impressed with my tenacity and talent, called in favors for session musicians when I couldn't handle a part on my own.

By the summer of 1984, I had a demo of five songs. By March of 1985, I had a recording contract with Capital Records, one of those serendipitous confluences of Uncle Oscar meeting someone who knew someone who knew an infamous hitmaker, who just so happened to be at Stephanie Katz's bat mitzvah, whose band had let me sing and play Taro's "Raindance," and just so happened to ask if I had ever considered making a demo, to which I just so happened to pull a cassette out of my purse, seeing as how I carried one with me everywhere because I just so happened to believe in both serendipity and preparation.

By Christmas of 1986, "Glossy" went to number one on the *Billboard* chart, and thanks to my very pink, very cosmetic video (and thank you, Sheila E, for paving the way with "Glamorous Life" and showing people like my father that women were kick-ass percussionists *and* frontwomen), I was officially a pop star.

Google "Joey 'Paisley' Parker" and you'll find a somewhat sanitized version of all this on Wikipedia, citing an in-depth interview I'd done with *People*, especially after MTV News reported that I'd filed a court petition to "divorce" Robert and Reneé Parker and legally live with Oscar and Mary Lou Parker as my guardians. I withdrew the petition to avoid the drama and distraction and legal fees, and moved out the day I turned eighteen, never looking back.

Like Aunt Mary Lou, my parents retired and relocated to Florida. But unlike Aunt Mary Lou, I never visited them. I didn't even miss them. But the kid in me had never stopped wishing things had been different, that I'd had parents who loved me. I had craved to be seen. All the sold-out stadiums in the world couldn't change the fact that the two people who brought me into this world had never really seen me.

Music saw me. Knew me. Loved me as much as I loved it. Music was my soulmate. That's what I told myself as a kid.

But some days I wondered if I needed more.

CHAPTER TWELVE

I needed to take this audition seriously. To say nothing of the fact that this was *Taro*—I also needed to be perfect.

I picked up the sticks and tested each snare and tom and cymbal and kick, slid on a set of headphones, and practiced for two hours straight—four-on-the-floor, Beatlesque fills, everything from Cream to Prince to Foo Fighters.

I felt rusty. Off the beat. Old.

I might not get this gig after all.

The band ambled into the studio around one-thirty the following day, guitar cases in hand. Michael, after testing them that day he stayed after the meeting, was content to use my keyboards. Ian brought coffee and Dr Pepper for everyone, and I was pleased he was respecting my no-alcohol rule. Since spring had officially arrived, we dined al fresco on the back deck after I set up a card table and some folding chairs, and spread out trays of kaiser rolls and cold cuts and condiments. My palms were sore from all the practicing I'd done the night before.

After a relaxed and perhaps prolonged lunch, we returned to the studio, where Garrett opened his case and pulled out a Rickenbacker bass guitar, the same one he played in "Last Call"—a 4001S, just like McCartney's during his Wings days. I fangirled more on the Ric than I ever would on Garrett. He pulled the strap over his shoulder and plugged into the amplifier as he began tuning and adjusting the amp's volume. The others followed suit and took their places, as did I.

"Let's hear what you've got, Joey," said Garrett.

I grabbed the sticks, slid on the headphones, counted off the beats by banging the sticks together, and broke into Tony Thompson's solo intro of the Power Station's "Some Like it Hot." Whereas the previous night I could feel frustration, perhaps even desperation to reclaim my timing and get every last beat precise, today I instantly came alive, as if I were back on stage. My heart kept the rhythm. My pulse picked up the pace. Garrett entered right on cue with the bass line as he and I made eye contact, and Johnny plugged in quickly to join Ian and Michael on the verse.

A shiver shot up my spine as Ian belted Robert Palmer's opening verse: "We've got to multiplyyyyy..." He meant business. We all did.

God, I wish I'd written that song.

For a band that had not played together or with me in years, we were remarkably in synch, save for a few botched notes and lyrics here and there. I'd missed the thrill of drumming with a band—like riding a roller coaster or a motorcycle—as adrenaline and caffeine coursed through me. Ian had matured from a exuberant, sometimes undisciplined singer to downright sexy, seducing an imaginary audience, its effect working on me. He'd finally decided to take voice lessons in his forties, I'd heard.

And Garrett. My God, Garrett. He puckered his lips and bobbed his head to the beat in full "bass face," eyeing me, the two of us in rhythmic harmony. We read each other perfectly, as if we'd known each other and had been playing together all our lives. It was exhilarating. Downright ecstatic.

Playing with Taro in the present moment, all grown up…It was like being in love. Like sex.

It was what being with Gav, even just talking to him, used to feel like.

It'd been a long time since I'd experienced those things, too. Too damn long.

Johnny improvised the guitar solo and laughed out loud when it had gone bad at the end, although he still managed to get right back into the chorus. Michael replaced the horn parts with a replicated Hammond organ. Garrett handled harmonies, while I doubled Ian one octave up on the chorus; I could still hit the high notes.

With the outro behind us, we all exchanged glances.

"Well," Ian said, catching his breath. "That fucking rocked."

"Yes," I said. "Yes, it did."

"Not bad for rusty," Garrett said to me.

Was he serious or sarcastic? Was he paying a compliment or leveling a criticism? I really needed to learn how to read him.

"I practiced last night," I confessed. "My arms are killing me already." The guys laughed.

This was what I'd wanted all along growing up—when I

saw the Beatles or Taro or INXS, I'd wanted to be part of that cohort, one in which each person and every instrument feeds off and listens to each other and volleys back and forth. I'd wanted bandmates. Hell, I'd wanted *siblings*. But few, if any, of my peers had been on my ability level, musically speaking. And no boys wanted a girl cramping their style, much less showing them up, especially on drums or electric guitar. Thing is, when I saw a band perform, live or on TV, be it the Beatles or Taro or INXS, I didn't just want to be Ringo Starr or Gavin Chandler or Jon Farriss. I wanted to be the bassist, the guitarist, the keyboardist, and the singer too. I wanted to be the songwriter, the arranger, the producer, and the engineer. I wanted to be Brian Wilson and Jeff Lynne. I wanted to be Carol Kaye and Carole King. I wanted to be Jon Ravelle and Edgar Naturally. I wanted to be *all* of them at once. And because no one wanted to or was able to play with me, I didn't have much of a choice but to be all of them.

It had been a lonely existence.

I'd wanted to be groundbreaking, too. I wanted to be part of that new wave sound, of Colin Thurston rather than David Foster. But I hadn't ridden in on that wave. I could emulate them, but I didn't want to. I wanted to be more than a copycat. That was why I called my album *Next Wave*. It was about taking everything I'd absorbed and running with it, making something that was, if not new, then *me*. Johanna Parker. Not Joey. Not Paisley. I'd come pretty damned close.

The heat of the glow radiated from my cheekbones, the musical high slow to wear off, and I hoped none of them were interpreting it as a fangirl moment.

But would that have been such a bad thing? Hadn't that been my dream at one time, to do exactly what we'd just done—jam and be peers and come out of it having had equal parts fun and respect? Couldn't I give that gift to my inner thirteen-year-old and be proud of it? Couldn't I revel in the dream come true thirty-six years later?

"Shall we do another?" Michael asked. "One of ours? 'Fever Dream,' perhaps?"

I looked at Garrett. "You up for it?" He knew what I meant. They all did.

He nodded toward me. "Count it off."

I clacked my sticks together, slower this time, and locked in on Garrett, who flubbed the first two bars but recovered quickly. Michael's part dominated the melody, and Ian and Johnny complemented each other with acoustic and electric guitars. "Fever Dream" was less a romantic ballad and more a sexy make-out song. No one would choose "Fever Dream" as a prom theme or a wedding song, but every girl would put it on a mix tape for her boyfriend.

Ian sang sensually, his voice and presence filling the room. It was electrifying to watch him, to watch all of them intuit each other's every move and tell. Yet it was also like playing at a memorial. Images and emotions flooded through me as I transported back to gawking at the television set, sitting directly in front of the screen despite your parents telling you it was bad for your eyes to do so, Taro performing "Fever Dream" on *The Tonight Show*, with Gav so alive and radiant, perched at his drum kit in the back and yet somehow still at the center of it all, and chills gripped my inner skin while my eyes misted over.

"Fever Dream" had always been one of Gav's favorites. It hit me as I recalled his telling Johnny Carson that. He'd told me during one of our multiple-hour long-distance phone calls.

And that's when I noticed Garrett making a concentrated effort to remain focused, to not get lost in the reverie of his twin brother. But it wasn't working. His mouth twitched, his eyes blinked rapidly, and when I caught the single teardrop roll down his cheek, I lost the beat, throwing everyone else off.

"I'm sorry," I said when the rest of the song structure collapsed and everyone stopped playing. "That was all me. Took my eye off the ball. I guess I really am rusty." I was trying to divert attention from Garrett and from the memories, from Gav being simultaneously and conspicuously present and absent. They all must have been thinking of Gav and having their own flashbacks, I surmised. How could they not?

"I can do better," I said.

Garrett stealthily erased the tear as he rubbed his eyes. "You're fine," he said brusquely. "Pick it up at the bridge."

I counted off again, and we resumed. When we finished the song, Garrett critiqued my performance. "You come in too fast at the chorus. Your fills are good, though."

I prided myself on my fills. Always have.

"You were a little wobbly there yourself," said Ian to Garrett, who glowered at him in return.

"We were all a little wobbly on that one," I said, cutting the tension off at the pass. "What's next?"

We played two more Taro songs, Stevie Wonder's "Superstition," then Michael suggested "Glossy."

I groaned. "That piece of shit?" The guys laughed. I counted off, sang the first verse and chorus, then motioned for Ian to take over. I never liked singing and drumming at the same time.

Besides, Ian sang it way sultrier than I ever did.

Why didn't my own song trigger any memories or emotions? Did all musicians feel that way about their work? Was Taro feeling that now as we played their songs?

Or maybe that classic impostor syndrome that lurked in

the deep recesses of every creator stole the spotlight: *What if it's not good enough? What if I am not, was not, and never will be good enough?*

When we finished, I wiped the sweat from my forehead and picked up a bottle of water beside me as I breathed hard, taking a long pull. The others followed suit.

"Talk about wishing you wrote something," Michael said when we finished. "Goddamn, that's a bloody sexy song."

Well, *that* turned me around. I swelled with pride and validation. There's no better feeling than a colleague—*your idol*—saying he wished he'd written your song. Especially one you wrote before you got your driver's license.

"Thanks," I said, beaming. "Means a lot to me coming from you."

"Are we done with the Mutual Admiration Society?" mocked Garrett. "Can we get back to playing? We all bloody need the practice."

I glowered at Garrett. *Thanks a lot, Cranky McBuzzkill.*

We completed our set with the Beatles' "Get Back" and, in homage to the iconic rooftop concert finale, I concluded with my best John Lennon voice impersonation: "I'd like to thank you all on behalf of the group, and I hoped we passed the audition." I glared at Garrett when I said "audition." He averted the wisecrack, removed the guitar strap from his shoulder, and excused himself to use the restroom.

At the end of the day, the guys left eager to return the following afternoon and start laying down tracks for new material. Garrett lingered.

"You played well today," I said.

"So did you," he replied. "You and I have chemistry, and we need that."

Chemistry. I had once looked up the word following one of my long-distance phone calls with Gav:

The identification of the substances of which matter is composed; the investigation of their properties and the ways in which they interact, combine, and change; and the use of these processes to form new substances.

And here I thought I'd been the only one feeling it today.

He quickly added, "You're not as good as my brother, though."

I took the criticism in stride. "Agreed."

"But you'll do for the album. You've got his style down. I even caught a few of his mannerisms in you. Don't know if it was deliberate."

"I used to try to play like him, yes," I replied. "I guess it's a part of me now."

He *is a part of me.*

"You have that same fire and enthusiasm that he did. Like you're playing a game or something."

My heartbeat sped and a flash of heat shot through me.

"Well, that is high praise," I said. "Thank you."

"Why did you let the record company change your name?"

The question, as well as the abrupt segue, caught me off guard. "Seemed like a reasonable concession at the time. I was so close to owning the world, you know?"

He looked around the room, as if taking note of his surroundings for the first time. "You got screwed, Paisley."

"Joey."

He donned a devilish grin. "I know."

I ignored the taunt. "Get some rest tonight," I said.

He scoffed. "Yeah, right." But he added earnestly, "You, too."

CHAPTER THIRTEEN

Two months into recording, and I was popping Advils with my coffee by noon.

For one thing, since the official announcement of Taro's making a new album and the crowdfunding campaign, Taro fans began showing up at my house at all hours. It wasn't hard to find; one Google search for Parker Studio and you'll get a freaking map.

First, they showed up at my front door. One of them brought her daughter dressed as a Girl Scout, under the guise of selling cookies. Then they attempted to trespass around back, where the private entrance to the studio is, but the locked gate and the alarm stopped them. One morning, I found two women camped out on my front lawn. My neighborhood had its own private security detail, and I had to ask them to park a car outside the house.

I mean, come on, people. You're middle-aged.

When a neighbor complained that a fan had wrecked his flowerbeds trying to get a snapshot of Johnny smoking a cigarette at the edge of my driveway, we decided to move the sessions to Garrett's house in East Hampton. Garrett, who'd been kvetching about the commute since day one, was especially on board.

Rick masterfully converted Garrett's piano room into our new recording studio—we rented a truck and hauled equipment from my studio to his, and we set up a control desk with a state-of-the-art Mac, software, and monitors.

"I'm kind of hating the guy right now for having this view," Rick said as he gawked out the window.

I laughed. "I thought you looked a little green today."

He turned to me. "This should be *your* house."

Had Gav been alive today, it might have been. Or one like it.

"I can barely take care of my own house."

"I meant—"

"I know what you meant," I said, then I backpedaled. "I'm sorry. I appreciate your sentiment. I guess I do have some regrets after all."

"Welcome to the club," he replied with a jovial pat on my back.

I smiled. "Do we get swag?"

He laughed. "I'll get on that."

Then there was Laurel, who was still hurt by my not introducing her to Taro. I had called her, trying to find a way to make amends.

"I'm really, really sorry, Laurel," I started.

"I get it," she said coldly. "You're a *professional*." I could almost see her air quotes.

"Did it ever occur to you that maybe I'm trying to protect you?" I said. "Because once you see how the sausages are made, the fairy dust disappears. I don't want you to lose that."

"So, what, you're telling me they're assholes or something?"

Garrett came to mind. *Well...*

"No. I'm just—look, isn't there some way we can work this out? After all, I gave you the news before anyone else. And considering you broke a trust by releasing those mixes when I specifically told you not to—"

"You're punishing me for doing what got you this amazing job in the first place? You are a special kind of obtuse, you know that? I've heard you complain over and over about how everyone shunned you after you got famous, but the truth is that you shut *them* out, Joey. And me."

Ouch.

That home truth was an arrow that took dead aim at and landed bullseye in my chest. And what poured out was the blood of my past. Of parents who met my interests with indifference; who responded to my bids for affection with a cold shoulder. Who criticized everything I said or did or offered as being insufficient, abnormal, or irrelevant.

Until my first royalty check arrived. Then they paid attention. Were it not for Uncle Oscar having the foresight to hire someone to look out for my financial interests, I wouldn't have put it past them to rob me of every last penny.

I had thought Uncle Oscar and Aunt Mary Lou had compensated for my parents' emotional abandonment—and they had. But not enough. Nothing really could. I now realized that, as a result, I'd held everyone in my life at arm's length. Gav was the only person I'd wanted to let all the way in. And he had opened his arms and invited me. "It's OK," he said before folding me into their warmth and safety. He had known me better than anyone. And now I wondered: Was that because of the letters and the phone calls, or the music? Were they the starting point, or had he known the moment we'd laid eyes on each other? Had I known even before that?

Would I have eventually shut him out, too?

"You're right, Laurel," I said softly, my head drooped in shame. "I'm sorry."

"I just miss the way it was when we were kids," she said.

Hell, I wasn't even a kid when I was a kid.

And come to think of it, when was the last time I was a *woman*? When was the last time I put on a dress, makeup, slingback shoes, and hit the town? Sure, those were all stereotypical, superficial female traits, but there had been a time when I did like those things, imagined myself doing them with Laurel when we grew up. Sitting in coffeeshops and drinking lattes; hosting book clubs with wine and cheese; retail therapy; double-dating.

But I wasn't a hostess and I wasn't a homemaker and I wasn't a shoe shopper and I wasn't a PTA president. I was never going to be, even if I had taken a more traditional career path. And yet, as was human nature, I just wanted to *belong* somewhere. Someplace where I didn't have to give away any part of my soul.

"I'll arrange a meeting," I offered. "When we're not as busy."

"Sure," she replied. I hadn't convinced her. Probably because I hadn't convinced myself.

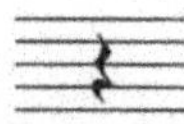

Since the sessions had begun, I'd been witness to one petty

argument after another, just as Michael had warned me. A documentary from 1985 had depicted Taro as a group of fun-loving yet disciplined kids in the studio, taking the craft seriously but not themselves. Michael told me that the marketing team had wanted to target the teen audience and didn't want to show any discord between the band members, so all footage of them fighting was cut.

I laughed. "I believed every minute of it."

He laughed as well. "Me, too."

Taro's recording process had changed a bit since those days. Back then, all five band members got songwriting credit, although according to Michael, Gav and Garrett had been the driving force behind pretty much every song. However, all five of them batted around ideas, contributed different parts and arrangements and tempos until they figured out what worked. Kind of like building a song with Legos. From there they'd rehearse each song live a few times before recording it track by track. Gav and Garrett were always together when they recorded their parts. Always. They'd insisted. "Johnny and I would lay down our parts, and then Benny would do the vocals. Jon and Edgar really knew how to get a good sound out of us," said Michael. "God, I miss those ol' buggers. I cried like a baby when Edgar died."

"So did I," I replied. "He's the reason I became an engineer in addition to being a producer."

The band members each had a handful of songs they'd written, and each threw two or three into the ring for consideration. Garrett had been opposed to this process; I suspected because he didn't have many (if any) to contribute. He also proposed doing a couple of covers, yet the band unanimously and adamantly voted down every suggestion he made.

"If we're going to cover anything, it should be 'Glossy,'" Michael said. "Benny really nailed it that day."

The suggestion was practically surreal. And yet, if you asked me to compile a list of people I wanted to cover any of my songs, I probably would've put Taro at or near the top.

"As flattered as I am, and as much as I agree that Ian did in fact kick ass, I still think original music is the way to go," I said.

"Crawler," Garrett mumbled.

Michael glared at him. "Seriously?"

"Creeper. Ass-licker."

Ian chimed in, "I believe the American term is 'suck-up,'" although he seemed to be teasing Garrett more than Michael. Or me.

"Are you two going steady now?" Garrett said to Michael and me. "Does Melinda know?"

"Sod off, Garrett," Michael said.

"Guys, please," I said, growing impatient, not to mention embarrassed.

"It's not a bad idea, actually," Ian said. "Doing 'Glossy,' I mean."

"It's over-saturated," I said.

"We could do it live," suggested Johnny. "Janet's team is planning the tour as we speak."

"Absolutely," said Michael. "Ease into it after 'Panic Button.' It's got the same time signature."

"Can we please finish this album before we start making bloody set lists?" Garrett barked.

"Right," Ian said. "I've got a new song. It's called 'Sod Off, Garrett.'" Everyone, myself included, cracked up. Everyone but Garrett, that is.

And that was how it went. Garrett against the world. It became clear that among the many upsets caused by Gav's death, the balance of power in the band had been one of them. It had always been Garrett and Gav vs. Johnny and Michael, with Ian as the tiebreaker. One of the reasons making *Been Too Long* had been such a nightmare, Michael had confided in me, was that Garrett no longer had his ally, his partner in crime. Jon and Edgar had known how to handle them. Jon especially had parented them. Gave them each a credible voice and validated their opinions and talents. But he also put his foot down with them, told them to sit down and shut up when they started throwing tantrums. Even overrode them on some of their decisions. He'd needed to be a parent—they'd all been so young, and some them hadn't gotten much parenting or discipline at home.

But here they were now, still acting like a bunch of children. The latest blowup was over a simple guitar chord that Garrett wanted in the bridge of one of Johnny's songs.

"It's a *diminished seventh,* you wanker!" Garrett yelled at Johnny at full volume. "Learn your bloody scales!"

"I know the bloody scale, and I know the bloody chord!" Johnny hollered back. "But it's a pop record, not a jazz solo!"

"Right, God forbid we make a pop record that's, you know, *good* for a change," said Garrett.

"The C-minor is fine, Garrett," Michael said.

"Spoken like a true Julie," said Garrett, his derogatory term for musicians who were classically trained at the famous Julliard School of Music. Michael wasn't one of them, but he might as well have been. "God forbid we stray from the technically correct into something exciting. IT IS NOT FINE," he thundered. "IT'S BLOODY BORING!"

"Oh, for fuck's sake," I said, exasperated.

Johnny forcefully removed his guitar strap from his shoulder and set the instrument in its holder.

"Are you leaving?" said Garrett, baiting him.

"I'm going to throw you through that bloody glass if you don't knock it off!" Johnny yelled, pointing at the picture window.

I stood up. "ENOUGH." I turned to Johnny. "You. Go cool off. Jump in the pool or the ocean or something. Watch out for jellyfish." I turned to Garrett next. "You. Into the kitchen with me." Then to Ian and Michael. "You. Don't say or do anything to piss me off in the next thirty seconds." Finally, to Rick, I said in as calm as voice as possible, "Can you find me some Advil, please?"

"Sure," he said before he muttered under his breath loud enough for only me to hear, "Can you find me a flamethrower?"

Bless Rick. He stood and set off in search of a medicine cabinet.

I pushed Garrett in the direction of the kitchen. Once there, he leaned against the island. I retrieved a tumbler from one of the cabinets, filled it to the top with water, and took a sip. Then I approached Garrett and threw the water at his face. He grimaced from the shock as well as the impact while I refilled the tumbler.

"Bloody hell," he said as he wiped his eyes, water beads dripping down his face and from the ends of his hair.

"Are you done?" I said. "Are you done being an asshole? Because honest to God, I can't take another minute of this. None of us can. One of them is going to walk out for real if you don't cut the crap, Garrett, and when they do, I'm going to follow right behind them."

"This is how we work, pretty girl," he said. "Don't like it? Then—"

Before he had a chance to finish his sentence, I threw the second serving (of water) in his face.

"Mother-fff—stop it!"

"I am *not* your pretty girl. I am your producer and your colleague. Stop acting like a fucking child and I'll stop treating you like one. And show me some goddamn respect."

This was what happened when I worked with certain guys. I swore and cursed and got in their face, especially when they condescended or were outright misogynistic to me. After all these years, I was tired of it. *This is why it's your last album,* I told myself. *Because you don't need this shit anymore. You never did.*

"Stop taking their side all the time!" Garrett screamed. "I need someone on my side! *I NEED SOMEONE ON MY SIDE!*" His face crumpled up, and he buried it in his hands and cried.

It was about Gav. It was always going to be about Gav.

I silently chided myself. I should have known. I *did* know. Because it was my job to know.

I calmed my breathing and remained still, allowing him a moment. He composed himself and fixed his focus on the tumbler.

"I am on your side," I said, my voice soft, gentle. "When you're here and you're fully present and you're all about the music, then I am on your side. Every time. But when you're demeaning and bullying everyone in sight and fighting them at every turn not because they made a bad musical decision but because you want to, then I'm out."

We were both taking slow breaths now.

"God, I want a fucking drink," he said more to himself than me. "Or ten."

I should have known that, too.

"Have some water," I said, and broke into a giggle following a beat. Thankfully, he joined me. The levity cut the tension.

Yet I segued to serious after another beat. "Do you need to call someone? Go to an AA meeting?"

He waved me off. "Later." Then he finally made eye contact, solemn and contrite. "I'm sorry about the *pretty girl* remark. You're not. I mean, you *are* pretty, but…oh, fuck it."

Another laugh escaped me, and my face flushed. I was dressed in faded jeans, a heather gray T-shirt that read FRIENDS DON'T LET FRIENDS CLAP ON ONE AND THREE (a birthday present from Rick a few years ago), and my beloved Sketchers. Wisps of hair fell out of my ponytail.

Yet Garrett didn't say I *looked* pretty…

When was the last time I *felt* pretty?

Gav had said I was beautiful. Called me "darling."

But this time, it was *Garrett* whose words made me quiver.

To my surprise, he leaned in to me, arms open, and pulled me to him in an embrace. I couldn't recall ever hugging someone I'd worked with, other than a hello or goodbye at the beginning or end of a session. But he did, and a surge raced through me, locking me to him. His body emanated so much heat it practically stifled me, made me break into a sweat. Or was peri-menopause making an uninvited appearance?

Dammit. I do not want to be feeling this.

"It's so hard," he said with a sniffle. "Doing this without him."

"Say his name," I said. "You've got to start saying his name again. It's hard doing this without *Gav.* I know it is. But it's harder doing this"—I gestured between us—"with you. It's no fun."

"I can't have fun without him."

"Have you tried?"

He looked at me, perplexed, as if no one had ever asked him the question before. As if he never even knew it was an option.

"Because you can," I said. "More importantly, you're *allowed.* And you need to. That's the way of the world. Ebbs and flows." I turned to the kitchen window and pointed toward the ocean, majestic and reassuring. "It's right outside. Learn from it. Draw strength from it."

He stared at it, as if caught in its spell, before returning his gaze to me.

"That's not all," he said. He opened his mouth, about to elaborate, but something stopped him.

"What?" I said.

His demeanor changed. "I'm sorry. Really. I'll stop being a git and I'll go and apologize to the others."

He padded out of the kitchen, ignoring the splotches of water on the floor. No way was I cleaning that mess up, too.

I lingered behind to look at the ocean. *You should take your own advice*, I heard. The voice wasn't mine.

CHAPTER FOURTEEN

Summer was in full swing, and so were we. Things had improved considerably in the weeks after the blowout and my moment with Garrett in the kitchen. We'd already finished four songs and were pleased so far. Buoyant. Catchy hooks. Doubled vocals and harmonies. Good sound. The guys were impressed with how meticulous I was about documenting every detail—the location of every mic, the level of every amplifier, and the make and model of every instrument used. This was a page out of Edgar Naturally's playbook; he had followed in the footsteps of the Beatles' engineer, Geoff Emerick. I couldn't keep up with the mail that cluttered up my dining room table, but ask me about a session from June 1989 and I'd know exactly where to find the binder that stored the notes and turn to the exact pages.

Rick was a godsend—down to earth with the band

members while still being a stickler for detail. Plus, his ear was impeccable. Our trust and respect and admiration and friendship were mutual. And, of course, it was about me giving up control—when you work alone for so long and do so much yourself, it's hard to hand the reins over to someone else.

"It's your desk," I said. "I trust you."

"That's why you're who you are," he said.

Best of all, I'd stopped feeling like I needed to prove myself and was trusting my instincts. Not that I was typically addled with self-doubt or a lack of confidence; but working with Taro was messing with me in that I wanted to get it more right than I'd ever wanted to get anything else right. As much as I told myself that this was just like any other gig, I knew there was at least one person I wanted to please: Gav. And although I was never really one for spiritual connections—I neither believed nor disbelieved in a deity, or universal force, or whatever you wanted to call it—since we started this album, I had found myself looking for some sign that Gav or Edgar even Uncle Oscar approved of our progress.

Who was I kidding—I wanted to please Garrett, too. All these years later, and I still wanted his approval. His blessing. And that was messing with me even more.

Maybe I finally trusted myself because they so willingly trusted me. Maybe they wanted to get it just as right, for the same reasons I did.

Or maybe it was the other way around. Maybe they trusted me because I trusted myself.

Perhaps what surprised me most was how much I loved playing drums with the band. Garrett and I sharpened our mental communication with every eye contact and interplay. Moreover, I could see his confidence in me—in our rapport—strengthening with every session, his willingness to allow someone that wasn't Gav into his aura. And the others took to my style as well.

Playing with Taro just plain felt good.

One afternoon, we decided to take some time off and wound up lounging around in Garrett's TV room, watching a tennis match the week of the Wimbledon tournament, when Garrett turned to me. "Did you know Gav and I wanted to be professional tennis players?"

The others continued watching as if they hadn't heard him, likely because this was old news to them. But my jaw dropped. Gav and I had discussed a great many things during our abridged courtship, but that wasn't one of them. Had he just not had a chance to get to it? Did he consider it unimportant?

"No, I did not know that," I said. I suddenly wondered what else I didn't know, and why I had assumed I'd known everything.

"We wanted to be football—sorry, *soccer*—stars too, but we were completely inept. We'd started playing tennis when we were six. Even took lessons at school. We competed in doubles tourneys and won a lot. Gav was better than I was, of course. He won a lot of singles matches, too."

"Yet you became pop stars instead. Why is that?"

"Pop stars get more girls."

I rolled my eyeballs.

"Do you still play?" I asked.

He shook his head. "One of the reasons we'd bought this house was because it came with a tennis court. But then… well, it's not a game for one."

Was *that* why I had never considered living anywhere else? Why bother when your future wrapped his car around a telephone pole? I'd been so quick to judge Garrett for giving up on everything and everyone he loved, but hadn't I done the same thing? I'd thought I had stayed true to myself by staying with the work all these years. But had I done nothing more than hide behind it?

"I used to play tennis, too," I said. "At school."

"Is that so?" he said, a lilt of pleasure in his voice.

"I gave it up early on. I was too busy with music lessons and practice and helping my uncle at his store." The memories flooded me as I spoke. When I wasn't at lessons, I was practicing. When I wasn't practicing, I was learning how to write and record songs.

Things hadn't changed much thirty years later. No wonder I didn't have any friends besides Laurel, and that lifeline had continually frayed.

"How sad for you," said Garrett. I think he had genuine empathy, despite the patronizing tone.

"But I loved watching the U.S. Open on TV. The only free time I carved out was when I used the side of the house as a wall—much to my parents' dismay—and hit a tennis ball against it with a racquet I bought at my Uncle Oscar's sporting goods store. I pretended I was playing against Martina Navratilova."

I didn't splurge on much when my records went to number one. But the courtside seats during Pete Sampras's first U.S. Open championship match in 1990? Worth every penny.

"Gav and I played against Martina at a charity game. The two of us against her. She creamed us."

I laughed. "Yeah, she creamed me even in my pretend games."

"Would you two shut it?" said Ian, throwing pretzels at us. "We're trying to watch the bloody match."

Garrett threw popcorn back at him. "Sod off, Benny, this is my house!"

"You're yapping like two kids at a slumber party!"

The fight escalated to Garrett taking hold of a throw pillow and hurling it at Ian's head.

"Right," I said, "that's way more mature."

Ian flung a pillow at me, and the next thing I knew we were all in the midst of a pillow war. I couldn't remember the last time I'd laughed so hard, or felt like a kid at…well, a slumber party. Definitely not typical band-producer behavior. In fact, I'd never before spent so much time in such close quarters outside the studio with any client.

And Taro was my client. This was a gig. I had to remind myself of that.

A fabulous, dream-come-true gig.

A couple of days later, when I arrived at Garrett's early in the morning (I always started working well before the others—listening to the previous day's efforts, setting up the mics, overdubbing a guitar track with synths), I found a brand new, top-of-the-line tennis racquet on the piano bench, with a red bow on the handle.

"I figured you and I could start playing to blow off some steam. And I could lose a few pounds," said Garrett, patting his belly like dough. Sounded like a muffled bongo.

And yet, an impulse to move into him, feel that belly pressed against mine, surged through and startled me.

"Thanks," I said. "That would be great."

Fifteen minutes into our first game, we were both gasping for breath, groaning as we stretched and massaged our stiff, aching muscles. None of our point plays lasted for more than a few volleys, until our final one, which we managed to sustain for two minutes. We quit ten minutes later. By mid-July, however, we were playing every morning for a good sixty to ninety minutes. Being so close to the ocean kept morning temperatures cool, albeit humid.

Dare I say, being with Taro day in and day out was increasingly like being in a family. I tried to ignore the fact that I had allowed myself to cross a boundary I'd never crossed before. I was *close* to these guys. For the first time in a long time, I felt as if I had friends aside from Laurel and Rick. Brothers. People who *got* me and liked me. Not Paisley Parker the pop star. Not Joey Parker the producer and engineer. But *me*. Johanna. We all enjoyed each other's sense of humor and made each other laugh. We'd crowd around the enormous island rather than sitting at a table in Garrett's kitchen, scarfing slices of pizza over the box, and convene to the TV room after a long or arduous session to watch movies or classic TV sitcoms like *Gilligan's Island* or *Bewitched*, anything that required as little brain activity as possible. Sometimes I was there so late that I stayed overnight in one of the guest rooms, too tired to make the two-hour trip back to Port Washington. Between the morning tennis and the late-night sessions, I packed an overnight bag and kept it with me. Michael taught me how to properly play Ray Manzarek's organ solo from The Doors' "Light My Fire." Johnny taught me how to nail the opening chord/strum of the Beatles' "A Hard Day's Night." I taught them the theme song to *The Odd Couple*. If we were between takes or fixing an equipment issue, we'd make up lyrics for Billy Joel's "We Didn't Start the Fire," most of them profane. Ian always came up with the best ones.

Whenever I was creatively blocked, I'd take a long shower. But now that I was spending so much time in East Hampton, I'd go for extended walks on the beach, and by the time I returned I'd have figured out how to get the right sound for a synth part or fix a chord progression in a song's chorus.

Sometimes snippets of music came to me in the middle of a game with Garrett, or during an episode of *The Brady*

Bunch. When I walked, I'd hum melodies into my smartphone or dictate new lyrics or arrangements, until Johnny started joining me. One time all five of us covered at least two miles of beach at sunset, while Rick volunteered to stay behind and fix a glitch in Pro Tools. (I also knew he worked better in such situations when he had no distractions or people looming over his shoulder.)

Occasionally, it hit me: *This is my job.* My passion. My love. I'd never desired to be a parent, but I nurtured the creative process of an album. I marveled at its maturation, was delighted by its secrets and surprises, and praised its mistakes as much as its triumphs. I celebrated its birth into being.

I'd never wanted to do anything else or be anything else. Even when teachers and guidance counselors politely urged me to "find a profession to fall back on," I would retort, "Would you ever tell that to someone who was certain they wanted to be a doctor or a lawyer?" Of course, the answer was always, "Well, those professions make money." To which I would staunchly declare: "*I* will make money." I'd never doubted it.

I'd desired stardom, too. I'd just never known it came with costs. No one ever does until the bill arrives and you have to pay.

And yet, the reason this was my final album was that I couldn't make a living anymore. The crowdfunding effort had already exceeded Taro's target goal—but was this going to be the future of financing in the music industry? Was Paul McCartney going to make a video—*"for five thousand dollars, you get to have fish and chips with me at the pub"*?

There was still money to be made in touring, but what were you going to play on tour if you could no longer afford to make records? Who would cover the costs of travel and lodging and everything else? Did I even want the grind of a tour at age fifty? Sure, McCartney could do it in his late seventies, but McCartney had first-class accommodations and sold-out stadiums and arenas. What kinds of venues could I fill, other than '80s festivals and nostalgia cruises and the like?

And what would happen when this album was finished? Would it be like any other gig, where the artists went their way and I went mine? Could I go back to my solitary existence?

I didn't want to.

And I didn't want to admit that I didn't want to go back.

I had options for life beyond music. But would I have joy? Would I have companionship? Because with every passing day, it was becoming increasingly clear that I'd gone without them for half of my life, and the hunger pains were panging louder every day. I couldn't be filled fast enough.

CHAPTER FIFTEEN

We decided to take the final week of August off, reconvening the day after Labor Day. Johnny, Ian, and Michael flew back to England to be with their families. Rick took his wife to Cape Cod. I visited Aunt Mary Lou in Florida.

It was nice to be mothered. Hearty home cooking. *Jeopardy!* in the evenings. She even insisted on making my bed.

"You complain about such chores while you're married, but there does come a point where you actually miss doing them for someone," she said.

"Having never had the opportunity, I'll take your word for it," I joked.

Aunt Mary Lou, however, took my quip seriously. "Is it something you want, Joey?" she asked.

"I've done fine without it," I said.

"That's not what I asked. I asked if it's something you

want. Do you want someone to cook for, make a bed, run an errand with?"

Had I ever wanted it?

I drew little shapes on the kitchen table with my finger, contemplating the answer.

"I don't know. On one hand, I've always been curious about what it's like. On the other hand, when I try to picture marriage and domesticity, it seems foreign to me. I just want…I want someone to…to *want* me. Not the way fans or the press or record companies wanted me. Not just the parts they can see. I want someone to see what's inside me and value it. Like you and Uncle Oscar did."

And Gav did.

Aunt Mary Lou smiled as her eyes became glassy. She put a warm, wrinkled hand to my cheek. "Dear Johanna," she said. "All you have to do is *show* what's inside."

Her declaration took me aback. "I thought I already was. With my music."

"No, dear. I'm not talking about your music. I'm talking about *you*. You show what you want others to see." She touched my hand. "I'm not saying that in a critical way. You learned it early on. It was self-preservation."

My vision blurred with tears. "Then how and where and when am I supposed to learn otherwise?"

"Same way you learn everything else. *Practice*. You make the decision to be vulnerable, to risk getting rejected. And you will be. But it's OK. Rejection doesn't define you. And vulnerability is the gateway to the good. But you sometimes pass through it on a path of pain. You need both. That's what life is all about."

My chest tightened with every word, which confirmed that Aunt Mary Lou was on to something.

"So, what—I let myself be a doormat?"

"Of course not! You have boundaries. But think about it—you've been rejected by record companies, audiences, critics. What made you keep going on stage?"

"I believed in my music," I replied. "I believed that it was good enough."

"And that *you* were a good enough musician. Now apply that to the rest of you. Believe you're a good enough Johanna."

If only I'd had a mom who'd told me that. The fact that I didn't was precisely why I'd needed to know, and why I had never believed it in the first place.

Despite the quality time with Aunt Mary Lou, I ached to be reunited with Michael, Ian, Johnny, and even Garrett—dare I say, *especially* Garrett, although I could barely admit it to myself, much less to anyone else. And that's when I realized how right Aunt Mary Lou had been. I couldn't even show *me* what was inside of me. If I couldn't face how I felt about these guys who were getting under my skin, then what chance did I have with romance? It was much easier, and perhaps more familiar, to put it in the music, just within reach.

When work resumed and I showed up at Garrett's and let myself in (he had given me the security code to the gate and a key to the house months ago), I found the band huddled around the kitchen island, a spread of bagels before them, just as Garrett finished bragging about the last threesome he had. (I didn't want to know what had prompted that conversation.) My gut clenched, and my face went hot; I steamed as if he was referring to a party I hadn't been invited to. Why should I care how he gets his rocks off? And why was I feeling so prudish all of a sudden?

They all clammed up the moment they saw me, which incensed me even more.

"Hey, Joey!" said Michael. "Welcome back. We missed you."

We missed you. The words should have elated me, but instead they sent me into a tailspin.

I homed in on Garrett. "Just curious: Did you sleep with those women because you're a guy, or because you're famous? I mean, would it have occurred to you to have a threesome if you were, say, an accountant?"

The bandmates exchanged nervous looks. "It's the first part of the other threesome," Garrett said matter-of-factly. My glower prompted a clarification. "Sex, drugs, and rock 'n' roll. It just sort of goes with the job description."

"I never behaved that way," I said. "I got offstage and went straight to bed—without taking anyone with me."

"That's because you were—" Garrett cut himself off.

Yet again the ugly memory, hard as I've tried to suppress it all these years, shot into the forefront of my brain and passed before my mind's eye, like an embarrassing clip from that old 1970s TV show *This Is Your Life*.

I glared at Garrett with laser-beam precision, so deadly the room went silent, tension filling in like smog.

"Say it, Garrett," I said. "You were going to say *fat*. I didn't get laid back when I was famous because I was too fat. Hideous. No one wanted to sleep with me, even for my fame or my money."

We locked eyes in a defiant showdown, a game of chicken. He said nothing.

"You made it clear that night, too."

"What are you going on about?" he asked.

"You know," I said. "*That* night."

And then the memory tumbled out of me and became real all over again:

Nineteen ninety-one. Backstage at the Grammys. Radio City Music Hall. My favorite place to play a show. Garrett and Gav were to be presenters and were already a little soused. I played no role in the ceremonies that night; I was backstage because I still had the clout to get backstage and because Gav wanted me there. Gav pulled me into a nook, seemingly oblivious to the surrounding flurry of movement and momentum, and kissed me.

Not a slobbery, intoxicated kiss. But sober. Lucid. A split second of clarity and alignment. An eternity of knowing. Soft and gentle and tender to the touch.

Time stopped. Motion stopped. All I could see were his eyes glistening, starlit, in perfect harmony with mine.

"I love you. Forever," he said, his smile a bouquet, every word a fragrant rose.

I took in a breath. "Please," I beckoned. "Please don't say something like that when you're drunk."

"No," he said. "This is me. I'm quitting the booze. Right now. I mean it. Even if it means giving up everything else, too. You're the one I want. Every night. Every day." He leaned in closer. "You're my favorite person, Johanna."

I believed him. I believed him because I could see it. Could feel it like an electrical current transferring from me to him, circulating throughout my body.

"I want you," I said just above a whisper. "I want everything."

And that's when Garrett sidled up to us.

"You know, Paisley," he slurred, "you'd could have bedded both of us had you just stayed away from the buffet table, you cow."

I had been called many things in my life. Nerd. Butch. Fat. I'd been accused of not writing my own songs. Of not being worthy of the fame and accolades I'd received.

I'd been all but disowned by my parents before I officially disowned them.

But nothing had cut me so deeply as Garrett's utterance of the word *cow*. Nothing had made me feel more ugly, stupid, or worthless. Nothing had made me feel more ashamed or self-loathing. Nothing had made me wish to be invisible, nonexistent.

Because the truth was, as in love as I was with Gav, I wanted to love Garrett, too. I'd worshipped him musically. I wanted and needed his approval, and not only where his wombmate was concerned.

Next thing I knew, Gav mauled his twin brother, screaming at him, and Garrett threw inebriated punches.

"Don't ever speak to her again like that or I'll kill you!"

"She's ruined you! You're going to let her ruin us, too?"

"*You* ruined us!"

It's a surreal moment when you, a fading pop star, watch A-List celebrities pull apart a set of twin pop stars, one of whom you're madly in love with, the other of whom just demeaned you, then you witness security guards threaten to throw them out the backstage door.

And you were the one responsible for it.

It's further surreal to know, after the fact, that it was the last time you would see the love of your life. I told him I wanted everything. And instead I lost everything.

I left. Not just Radio City Music Hall but also the spotlight. From that night forward, I was permanently a studio musician, producer, and engineer. Pay no attention to that cow behind the mix desk.

Watch the video clip of Garrett and Gav's award presentation and you'll see identical twins, usually loose and free and jovial, standing at the lectern stiff and constrained and deadpan. The press attributed it solely to their being drunk—which, by then, they most certainly were. So much for Gav's promise to stop drinking.

The moment they fulfilled their obligation, Gav was gone. *Forever.*

"Joey..." Garrett started, but I cut him off and fired my next shot.

"You know what I think? I think you're a whore."

Never had I been so unprofessional. Or cruel, for that matter.

Garrett didn't even look mildly wounded. Instead, he *smirked.* "You sound awfully jealous, Joey. You sure you didn't fancy me even a *smidgen* back in the day?" He drew his thumb and forefinger close together at the word *smidgen*, gesturing a little squeeze. "Confused my twin for me?"

I fumed. "No. You know why? Because even then I knew you were as big an asshole as you are now."

Then he laughed—he *laughed*—not at what I said, but at *me*, and I stormed out.

"She's right, you know," I heard Johnny say before I was out of earshot.

Twenty minutes later, Garrett met me on the tennis court, thwacking a ball against a large plank he'd set up against the chain-link fence for those times he wanted to practice solo. The other guys had taken to playing handball against it during breaks. With each pounding I released a Serena Williams-esque grunt, expelling the anger not only from the last hour but also from thirty years ago. Plus, the secret admission that Garrett was right and I *was* jealous. Inexplicably jealous. Not that I'd ever want a threesome—*ick*—but that I had been increasingly connecting to Garrett in ways that were all too intimate. The communication from percussionist to bassist. The musical sensibility. The casual conversations we fell into at the end of the day. The way we complemented (and complimented) each other on the court as well as in the studio. It wasn't so much that we were playing against each other or with each other as that we'd been playing *for* each other.

This was what I was terrified to show—to myself, to the world, and most of all, to Garrett.

And yet, none of it could erase the past. And none of it could salve the wound he'd just inflicted again at the site of the scar.

"Your backhand has improved a lot since we started playing," he said after watching me for a few minutes. I ignored him as I served another ball at the wall, imagining his head in its place.

He didn't wait for me to reply. "So the consensus is that I'm an A-level asshole."

I kept my eye on the ball. "Consensus? More like unanimous."

"Point, game, set, match." He took a tentative step toward me when the ball careened over the wall and plopped into the pool. "I'm sorry, Joey. Really, I am. I was completely out of line. I guess sometimes it's hard to forget we're all grown up now."

You're in your fifties—when were you going to notice?

"Some of us more than others," I said. I released my grip on the racquet and let it clatter on the court before finally facing him.

"Can we be friends again?" he asked.

"You called me a cow that night," I said, a succession of tears cascading down my cheeks. "A *cow*."

He lowered his head in shame. "Honestly, Joey, I didn't mean anything I said that night. I—"

"You think that excuses you?"

"No. I'm sorry. I really am. I'm sorry for anything and everything I said and did. Especially that night."

His apology sailed past me. "It's wankers like you that made those wanker record company executives refuse to put my photo on my own freaking album covers, or use me in my own music videos from the neck down. All they saw and heard was a cow. Just like you did."

And right there on the court, I wept for that girl who just wanted to make music. Who wanted to make *magic*. Make magic with her idols. With the love of her life, for the rest of their lives.

And perhaps I had even wanted to make my parents love me and be proud of me.

But it went even deeper than that. *Believe you're a good enough Johanna,* Aunt Mary Lou had said.

All my life, regardless of my weight or size or talent or fame, Garrett's choice of word embodied how I'd always felt inside.

I wept even harder for *that* girl.

"I'll bet Jon Ravelle never blubbered like this. Or Jeff Lynne. They didn't have to. The artists they worked with never called them cows. Never looked at or treated them like they were little girls. Never called their talent into question. They had the right anatomy."

"Joey, please. I *do* respect you. You have to know that. I just…"

I waited for him to finish his sentence.

"I'll just shut up now." He paused for a beat. "Except to say this. I will be sorry for that night for the rest of my life." He spoke slowly, sadly.

He dropped his head again and turned on his heel and left me alone. I cried myself out, left the racquet to bake in the sun, went inside to shower, and re-entered the piano room-converted-studio, where Taro and Rick were waiting, pretending as if today was just another day and I was just another producer.

"Let's get back to work," I said. "We've already wasted enough time."

CHAPTER SIXTEEN

By October, we were seeing the light at the end of the recording tunnel—we had fifteen tracks either finished or close to finished, and even though all fifteen weren't going to make the final cut, we were pleased with the surplus. The songs were exactly what Taro and I had wanted them to be at the onset: Funky. Danceable. Catchy hooks and lyrics. Simultaneously contemporary and timeless. Just a little retro for flavor and fan nostalgia, but subtle. Ballads that were sweet but not syrupy. Romantic, but not I-Will-Always-Love-You power anthem. Ian's voice was seasoned, controlled, better than I'd ever heard him. Johnny, who had never fancied himself a guitar hero, wowed me at every session. Michael, always the virtuoso, was one of the most underrated keyboardists and musicians in the business, possibly because he was also one of the most fashionable.

And Garrett? Garrett was still a master craftsman. Still a visionary.

And, if I do say so myself, I didn't suck, either.

Ever since our post-Labor Day blowout, Garrett and I had pretty much kept our noses to the grindstone and took out any lingering aggressions on the tennis court. We sparred when the weather permitted and spoke little during our games. And yet, a conversation seemed to be taking place with every volley, as if we were slowly, silently making peace with each other and our past. Wiping the slate clean. Accepting that neither of us now was the same person from thirty-something years ago.

Perhaps Gav was refereeing courtside, reminding us to keep our eyes on the ball rather than the score.

October also brought my fiftieth birthday front and center. Normally, I wasn't sentimental about birthdays—I'd never had parties as a child, mostly because my parents believed them to be a waste of time, and when Uncle Oscar and Aunt Mary Lou took it upon themselves to hire a party planner and surprise me with a Sweet Sixteen *event* in Manhattan after the success of "Glossy," complete with celebrity special guests, the attention felt downright awkward. But this year was different. I don't know what made fifty the milestone that differed from thirty or forty, but nevertheless I felt like I'd arrived at a crossroads. If only I knew which direction to take as the Taro album wound down and the *what's next* phase of my career loomed.

This time, I wanted a party. Or, at the very least, a small celebration.

My birthday was on a Saturday this year. In addition to hiring professional cleaners to do a run-through, I invited the band, Rick, and Laurel to my house for a catered dinner. After I contritely reached out to Laurel several times, she finally accepted my olive branch.

"You were right," I said. "I've been a lousy friend over the years. It got easy to keep everyone at an arm's length, especially once I went into the fame bubble. But I want to do better. I really do. And I want to start by inviting you to my birthday party. You, me, and the guys."

"Wait—what guys?" she asked, already knowing the answer.

"Ian," I said, starting with her favorite. "And Garrett and Johnny and Michael."

"And no one else?" She percolated with every word.

"Just my buddy Rick, the engineer who's been working on the album with us."

"Spouses and significant others?"

"Optional, but unlikely. Michael's and Ian's wives are in London. I'm pretty sure Rick is bringing his wife."

She didn't scream this time, likely because she was at work.

"How could I say no?" she said, playing it cool, yet her voice still quavered with excited anticipation.

"Will you need a sitter?"

"The girls are old enough to be on their own. Besides, Bill will be home."

Apparently, she'd already chosen her spouse option. I couldn't blame her. I don't think I would want my spouse observing me with the guys I'd lusted over throughout my adolescence and even well into adulthood.

The band, however, had other plans. "Catered dinner?" said Ian. "Blimey, Joey, you really don't get how this rock star thing works. You are not hosting a catered dinner for your fiftieth birthday."

"Why not?" I asked. "What's wrong with that?"

"Because we've already made arrangements for a celebration in Manhattan."

Well. OK then.

At least my house got cleaned. And perhaps I could treat Laurel to a catered dinner for *her* fiftieth birthday the following month.

It's possible that the Manhattan option was prompted more out of stir-craziness than generosity—we'd barely been anywhere beyond Garrett's house or my own—but I was all too happy to accept it. Laurel insisted that we shop for new dresses and get mani-pedis and hair and makeup done. I hadn't fussed, or been fussed over, like that since the days of photo shoots and videos and TV appearances and concerts. She helped me select a cocktail dress that was neither an earthy-crunchy tea-length nor a fifty-year-old-embarrassing-herself-wearing-a-twenty-year-old's mini-dress. I'd never felt comfortable in dresses, probably because I'd been a chunky kid and dresses seemed to accentuate rather than hide that chunkiness. Moreover, I'd never felt *feminine* in dresses. In the heyday of my fame, I'd been chastised no matter what I wore. Getting out of the limelight meant, thankfully, getting out from under the microscope of media and consumer cruelty, which was tame then compared with the present day. Besides, being in the studio for long hours required function over fashion, and eventually I morphed from leggings and boots and blazers to jeans and T-shirts and Sketchers. Stopped wearing makeup, too. Even after losing weight, a sexier wardrobe that showed off my body seemed pointless. I wasn't in the studio to pick up guys, after all. I was there to work. What I wore didn't have any effect on the music I made.

Or did it?

I'd wanted to be taken seriously, yes. But was it possible I also wanted to remain invisible post-fame, especially after Gav died?

The truth was that while talent and luck went a long way in this business, so did *charisma*. It took on different forms, be it four mop-tops in simple suits and Nehru collars, a shaggy-haired, bespectacled hippie who belted out the blues, a guitarist and bassist who defined disco, five teens on the cutting edge of fashion as well as sound, an MTV performance in a wedding dress that conquered the world, or a garage band in flannel shirts and ripped jeans that sparked the next genre in music. Since the age of the Internet, the trends shifted as quickly as the wind. But nevertheless, you could count on their presence.

Despite the personal stylist at Nordstrom gushing about how fabulous I looked, I felt gawky, graceless, and like a kid playing dress-up in my mother's clothes. That is, until I found *the* dress. Sheath. Red, like Garrett's Beamer. Scoop-neck, revealing just a tease of cleavage. Cap sleeve. And I knew, after hair and makeup and shoes, that it would be downright sexy. Hell, I felt sexy already. I couldn't remember the last time—if any—that I felt sexy.

In addition to all the pampering, I had fun with Laurel. It was reminiscent of our early teen years.

Rick agreed to meet us in the city rather than share the stretch limo the band reserved.

"Don't want to cramp your style," said Rick.

"Or maybe you don't want your wife in such close proximity to Ian and the rest of them."

He laughed. He also didn't deny it.

Laurel looked smashing in a black cocktail dress and stilettos. Her hair and makeup were flawless, her skin luminous, her body fit and in better shape than she'd been in her twenties. I opted for low-heeled but stylish slingbacks, not only to show off my painted toenails but also because I didn't want to walk like a klutz, especially given that it had to be at least twenty-five years since I'd worn anything with a heel higher than two inches. And with my hair dyed a rich espresso, pulled up into a French twist, professional makeup, and hands and feet sloughed and buffed and filed and lacquered (my hands were especially in rough shape; I didn't want to lose my callouses, but for once I wanted the hands of someone who worked with doilies rather than drums), I looked like…

Well, like a rock star.

Laurel shifted her weight from one foot to the other when she stood and fidgeted when she sat, trying to keep her composure but growing giddier with every passing second we waited for the limo—and the band—to arrive.

"Bill knows where you're going tonight?" I asked.

"I may have said we were going to see Taro *perform* rather than *go out to dinner with them*."

I laughed. "He knows I've been working with them, though, doesn't he?"

"Everybody knows you've been working with them."

The baby-faced assistant at Nordstrom probably didn't.

"Well, don't you think it's a little far-fetched that you'd be going to a concert when you look like you're dressed for a wedding?"

She waved me off. "Bill is clueless when it comes to such things. Where are we going, anyway?"

"Don't know. The guys didn't say. I think Ian made the reservation. Some hotshot restaurant."

Laurel clapped her hands in rapid succession. "I can't believe it!"

"It is pretty wild, isn't it?"

"I don't know how you work with them day in and day out without jumping their bones."

"I don't really think about that," I said.

Or rather, I didn't *let* myself think about that. I couldn't deny that I still found all four Taro members physically attractive after all these years. But over the last few months I'd come to develop more of a brother-sister relationship with Michael and Johnny. Besides, Michael and Ian being married was enough of a turnoff for me. Ian pretty much flirted with any woman who looked in his direction, but taking Garrett down that first day in the studio scared him straight, which had been the point.

That left Garrett.

With the band, I felt camaraderie. With Garrett, I felt chemistry. In the studio. On the tennis court. Even when we fought.

I couldn't avoid recognizing Gav in him—the deep-blue pools with the long lashes, the high cheekbones, the million-dollar smile (almost literally—he and Gav both had expensive orthodontic work done). Sometimes I'd watch Garrett while I drummed and he played bass—he still insisted on recording both parts together, just like he used to do with his brother—and I'd almost lose myself, and the beat, in a stare. The years gone by. His musical IQ, the kind you can't teach someone. The way he puckered his lips as he played and practically danced in place.

Why had I chosen Gav over Garrett all those years ago as the object of my teenage fantasies? I had to have seen something that went beyond the pin-up perfection. I remember writing about Gav in my diary: *I feel like I know what's in his heart.* I would imagine us sitting on a blanket under a tree somewhere, legs crossed, a picnic basket between us, talking for hours about everything and nothing. Our hopes and fears. Our disappointments and dreams.

And, it turned out, that's exactly what we did. That first date at the Palladium, I saw him shimmer upon the sight of me, as if he'd actually *read* my diary and agreed with it. As if he'd *planned* it.

If only we'd had more time.

Music is supposed to be timeless. It's supposed to make musicians immortal. (Hello, Wolfgang Amadeus Mozart.) But with Gav, it felt as if he'd been mummified in those albums, forever frozen at age twenty-four. Or like Edward the vampire in the *Twilight* series. The more time I spent with Garrett, however, the more I surmised that there wasn't only a lot of Gav in Garrett—there had been a lot of Garrett in Gav. I could see it now, in hindsight. A roll-off-the-shoulders mentality. A pragmatism that offset his creativity. And an ability to be introspective. Thing is, Garrett rarely allowed anyone to see those things. Perhaps those things had been mummified in him when Gav died.

What would life had been like had Gav not gotten in the car that night? How long would Taro have continued? Would *we* have continued? Would we have settled down, taken ourselves out of the spotlight? Would we have had kids? And how would Taro—especially Garrett—have reacted if we'd done that?

It was always frustrating to never be able to play the story out in full. I could only imagine how many times Garrett and Ian and the others ran those what-ifs and if-onlys through their head before remembering it was futile. Perhaps as many times as I did.

CHAPTER SEVENTEEN

It was still daylight when the limo pulled into the driveway, but the sun was setting fast. I opened the front door just as the driver ambled up the walkway to escort us to the car.

"Ohmigod, I think I need to use the bathroom!" shrieked Laurel. She scurried away and returned minutes later.

Even I was a little nervous, I'd realized.

The bandmates were getting rowdy and mockingly impatient. Geez, had they already started drinking? When the driver (named Nick; I asked) linked arms with Laurel and me, one on each side ("Lucky me," he said) and gallantly strode with us to the limo, the back doors and sunroof were open, and the band members were either standing up or halfway way out of them, whistling as they saw us. You'd think we were going to the prom.

And maybe we were. None of us, with the exception of Laurel, had a normal high school experience.

Or maybe it just goes to show how stir-crazy we'd all been.

"Oh my God, Joey!" exclaimed Ian. "Your hair is a different color! And you've got legs! And breasts! And dainty hands and feet! And might I say they are all rather divine."

Screw it. Let him flirt. Tonight, I was a woman, not a producer. I wanted to be sexy tonight. Fifty was sexy. Hell, fifty was goddamn fabulous, I decided.

Then I saw the look on Garrett's face—it was identical to Gav's when we met at the Palladium. Except Garrett looked more bewildered than anything else. As if he'd seen me somewhere before but couldn't quite place the face. And yet, he clearly was enamored.

He wasn't the only one.

I avoided direct eye contact with him and the rest of the band as I approached the car. They each donned designer suits and ties and sprayed their hair and arrived ready to pose for a photo shoot.

My God, they were gorgeous.

In fact, they looked like the Taro I'd fallen in love with in my youth, aged like a work of art. And let's face it: Ian Bensa, Michael Spaulding, Johnny Rogers, and Garrett Chandler were works of art. Their hair. Their faces. Their bodies. Their clothes. Their talents.

Yeah, I was so not a producer tonight, and they were not my brothers.

I basked in their attention. And dammit, I *wanted* it. Until that moment, I hadn't allowed myself to admit that I'd been thirsting for it—not necessarily theirs, specifically, but anyone's. The kind you feel on stage that has nothing to do with fame or success, but rather is something deeply personal, one-on-one. I'd rather get drunk on that than champagne.

And speaking of champagne, Michael and Ian had already

popped open a bottle and filled their flutes. Garrett and Johnny, who was also in recovery, drank mocktails.

I casually introduced Laurel to Ian, Johnny, Michael, and Garrett, and she did her best to be cool and collected, but the moment Ian kissed her on the cheek upon the greeting (I "let it slip" to Ian in the introductions that he was her favorite), she blurted out another "Oh my God" an octave higher than her normal speaking voice, almost sounding like one of The Chipmunks. How and why did Ian's wife stay married to him all these years? I certainly couldn't have. It was another reason I never married. Being around all those celebrities at the time, monogamy was a pipe dream, a fairy tale. Would Gav and I been able to have a "normal" life in that regard?

I thought about what Aunt Mary Lou had recently asked me: *Is it something you want, Joey?*

Ian served Laurel and me each a flute of champagne, and they toasted me.

"To our Joey, who singlehandedly saved our sorry selves from oblivion," said Ian.

They all erupted in a cheer.

Ian took a sip, and his eyes instantly misted over. "Seriously, love. We were done. You really did save us. Not just musically. We are alive again. *All* of us."

Garrett averted his gaze to the window upon Ian's emphasis of *all*.

With that, the celebration was reduced to whirring of the car's motor. Damn if Ian didn't bring all of us to tears. Because he was right. And I wanted to cling to it with my newly manicured hands.

"To aliveness," I said softly, verklempt. We clinked flutes and glasses, and when Garrett and I connected, he averted his gaze yet again. I practically read his mind: *All of us but one.* And the one might well have been him. Or Gav. Or the two of them together. Because in that twin way, two really was one.

"So, Laurel," started Michael. "Tell us what it was like to be an American teenage Taro fan." The bandmates followed suit and peppered Laurel with question after question:

"Which of us was your favorite?" asked Ian, obviously knowing the answer.

"Who had more posters on the bedroom wall—you or Joey?"

"Which one of us did Joey kiss the most?"

I pulled a face/palm, careful not to smudge my makeup but shielding my eyes so they wouldn't betray me with the answer. Yet I still caught Garrett smirking in protest. Ironic, considering he had taunted me with that very image.

Was it possible that he was jealous?

Of course, Laurel disclosed the truth. But at that moment I kind of wanted to pucker up with every last one of them, and that's what I was really afraid of revealing.

"Tell us your ultimate Taro sex fantasy."

"Oh, come on," I said in recoil. Laurel said she was going to have to drink a lot more to disclose it, and I hoped they wouldn't actually hold her to that. I knew the details of that fantasy.

The interrogation continued:

"Describe what Joey looked like as a little girl."

"Tell us something really embarrassing about Joey that will make her blush right now."

"Like none of this is making me blush?" I interjected.

"It's hard to picture you as anything less than studious and focused," said Johnny.

"Yeah," Ian chimed in, "we want to know fun Joey."

Now I was genuinely hurt. "I'm not fun?"

"You're not rock-star fun," said Ian.

"I don't even know what that means," I said. He must have had more champagne than I'd previously thought.

Laurel ignored my comments and replied to Ian. "Ohmigod, she was such a little geek. For one thing, she actually liked math. She even joined the math club in seventh grade."

My teacher Dave Angelique had told me students who excelled at math also excelled in music.

"Hey, music is what mathematics does on a Saturday night," I said, quoting Dave.

"Were you the teacher's favorite?" teased Garrett.

"Yes," answered Laurel for me. "All the teachers loved her."

"That's not true," I said. "They didn't love me when I started recording. My grades went down the tubes."

"They forgave you once you got a record deal," Laurel said.

"Right," I said, "and the entire student body suddenly wanted to be my friend. Same goddamned kids who used to egg my locker."

"No cursing in that dress," Ian said.

After crawling through typical New York traffic, we arrived at the five-star, fully booked restaurant teaming with VIPs and A-listers. Perhaps a place like this would have been my scene in the mid-late eighties had I been old enough, but even now I felt like a bit of an impostor. I ordered a cut of pork with a cherry-balsamic chocolate sauce that I thought was going to give me an orgasm right there at the table. The others bragged about their dishes, and at one point we passed plates around, giving each other sample bites. Ian, the foodie of the group, took over the wine menu as well. I'd already finished a glass in addition to the flute of champagne in the limo, but I couldn't help but feel like we were all torturing Garrett and Johnny. Especially Garrett. I leaned into him, seated next to me and uncharacteristically quiet, and said softly, "Are you OK with all this booze going around?"

He smiled politely and nodded. "Don't worry about me. Drink up."

"Are you sure? I feel like we're being disrespectful or insensitive."

"Not at all. It's your night, Johanna."

Johanna. Had he ever called me by my full name before? Especially with such sincerity, even tenderness?

"Johnny and I cleared it with Ian and Michael. We've got each other's backs tonight. Plus, I have my sponsor on call. Really, it's OK. I appreciate your asking, though."

What was life with a recovering alcoholic like day in and day out? I wondered. Was it just at parties that one had to be vigilant, or was it an everyday thing?

Come to think of it, what was life with *anyone* like day in and day out? How did couples divvy up chores or put up with each other's bad habits or sleep through snoring or tossing and turning? Who made the coffee in the morning? Who took charge of the bills? What did they talk about at mealtimes? What did they do when the kids weren't around? And what happened when shit really hit the fan? Funny, I'd never asked Laurel or Rick how it all worked. Never consciously observed Uncle Oscar or Aunt Mary Lou. They seemed to be in harmony; I never thought to ask how or why they were. Their harmony was enough for me; it's what I'd been starving for and what had been so conspicuously absent from my parents' marriage.

After dinner, Taro sidled up to the piano player, slipped him what I guessed to be a hundred-dollar bill, and took over his territory. They had the room's attention, including the staff, in less than a second.

"Right, so we're here to celebrate a special birthday. Miss Johanna Parker," said Ian as he pointed in my direction.

Again with my full name. I rather liked it.

I staved off the eyes-on-me and waves and polite applause, especially when Laurel let out a rather boisterous WOOT. "Now, some of you might know her as Paisley Parker, of 'Glossy' fame, but to us she is a producer and percussionist extraordinaire. She can do it all. But…can she do this?" Michael, at the piano, then broke into the key of A and a rousing version of The Beatles' "Birthday" ("none of that 'Happy Birthday' bollocks, and did you know it took two people to write that song?" I found out Garrett had said when they'd hatched the plan) with Garrett and Ian clapping to the beat in lieu of a drum, and Johnny singing a loud and comical "da na na na na na na na" where the guitar part should be. Ian belted the lead, with Michael and Garrett on backup vocals.

God, their energy. Their charisma. They exuded the exact same sex appeal in their mid-fifties as they'd had in their late teens. When performing in front of an audience—any audience, be it a sold-out crowd at Wembley or a room of restaurant patrons—they were simultaneously vivacious and smart and playful and captivating. What separates a talented musician from a star is that thing no one knows how to name but everyone recognizes the second they see it. Like the Beatles on *The Ed Sullivan Show* in 1964. In fact, that's what the A&R guys and the music journalists and the tastemakers and even the fans mean when they say, "You've got it." And the *it* is somehow understood.

Taro had it in spades. Still.

I had it, too, back in the day. Perhaps that's why, despite my body size, I still came away with successful tours and a string of hits.

As Taro sang and performed for me, I felt like a fan again. Moreover, I felt *special.* I basked in the presence of every note, half wishing I could join them. I was also proud. Watching the guys relish the spotlight, the participation, and the applause was akin to the pride and adoration I imagined parents had when their kid performed in a school play or piano recital or speech competition. The guys signed autographs on napkins for patrons and took selfies with wait staff. They posed for a photo with the executive chef, who had known in advance that the band was going to be there. "I was a fan back in the day," said the chef. "You guys were the best way to get girls."

Laurel captured the entire thing on her phone. "Don't worry, I won't upload this one to YouTube."

"Actually, I think you should," I said. Laurel raised her eyebrows at me, as if to say *who are you, and what have you done with Joey Parker?*

Johnny agreed. "We could use the press as well as the publicity. Let everyone know we're back. There's already been buzz thanks to the crowdsourcing."

"I have to admit the crowdsourcing was brilliant," said Ian. "I wouldn't want to fund every album that way, but we're very close to making a deal with Sony. That's how popular it's been."

"I donated a hundred dollars," Laurel bragged.

Ian toasted her. "We thank you from the bottom of our glasses," he said as he emptied his own.

Just as they finished, the executive chef personally delivered a fondant-covered vanilla-almond poundcake in the shape of a treble clef to me and topped with a single candle.

"Make a wish," Laurel touted.

"I am *not* blowing out that candle," I said.

"You have to."

"Laurel, you're the one that told me how unsanitary it is. Heck, you don't let your own kids blow out birthday candles."

"That's a thought that's going to stay with me forever," Garrett muttered.

"OK, fine. But you still need to make a wish," she said.

"How about gold and platinum sales of the new album," I said.

"Christ, those were the good ol' days," said Ian.

"Or one of everything from the Sweetwater equipment catalog," I added.

"Sod off with record sales and new gear," said Garrett. "Wish for something you wouldn't tell your mum. Or us, for that matter."

Oh.

I didn't even know how to put it into words. I wanted to say *a normal life*, but what was that, exactly? Was it the life I presumed everyone else had? Was it a soulmate? Was it parents who loved you? Was it an uncle who was still alive to see you do great things? Was it actual great things? Had anything I'd done since 1986 been *great*?

No, not normal. *Content.* I wanted to know what it felt like to truly know yourself in your own skin and be satisfied. I wanted to know what it was like not to have to try so hard to be all things for all people, or everything but what I most wanted, which was simply, *me*.

Or perhaps was it more of this—friends and food and dresses and laughter and singing together.

It was together. That's what I wished for. More *together.* A lifetime of together. With my true self as much as with a tribe.

With *a band.*

Using a spoon, I snuffed out the solitary candle, then cut the cake and doled out slices.

It's possible the poundcake with raspberry cream was even more divine than the dinner.

"I'm not sure that wish was valid without blowing out the candle," said Ian. Surprisingly, my spirits sank at his suggestion.

"I never considered you the superstitious type," said Rick.

"I love black cats, though," he replied.

After dessert, I stood up and excused myself to the restroom, and Laurel followed.

"This has been the best night of my life," she said when we reached the waiting room. She extracted a compact from her clutch and powdered her nose. "Seriously, didn't we have this exact fantasy when we were thirteen? You, me, and Taro partying in limos and fancy New York restaurants? Remember all those screaming girls who used to beg for just a wink in their direction? You just ate birthday cake with *Taro*! They all *sang* to you and then *hugged* you. *You!*"

Well, when you put it like that...

"And Ian kissed you on the cheek," I said. "Too bad you can't swab it for DNA and sell it on eBay."

"Don't tell my husband about that, OK? Because you know who I would rather be going to bed with tonight."

"Don't tell Ian's wife, either."

She sighed. "You are *so* lucky, Joey. You've got the most incredible life ever."

"What makes you think so?" I asked and tacked on, "I don't mean to be argumentative or ungrateful. I'm genuinely curious."

"You really don't think you do?"

"I guess I just never saw it that way. At least not since I left the limelight. Or before I entered it."

"Jo-Jo, you have more tenacity in your pinky than most people do in their entire bodies. You didn't just sing into your hairbrush, try out for the school band, and then go become a math teacher or something. You did exactly what you wanted to do, and you practically did it all by yourself at age fifteen. *Fifteen.* God, most kids don't even know what they want to be at fifteen. *You made an album that went to number one*, after everyone told you you couldn't because you were too young, too inexperienced, and too much of a girl."

"But anyone could have done what I did," I said. "You could have, Laurel, if you'd wanted to."

She looked at me, incredulous. "Are you kidding me? You're forgetting how my parents yelled at me—*yelled* at me—when I said I wanted to be a cake decorator. I wanted to go to culinary school, and instead they made me go to SUNY Binghamton and be a business management major. Told me I needed to get a good job in the city, whatever that is. Do you think I *like* being an administrative assistant? Do you think it's what I daydreamed about?"

When I turned fourteen, Laurel had baked me a chocolate cake from scratch and decorated it with a sea of M&Ms and a fence line of Kit Kats. She had seen a picture of it on the cover of a *Good Housekeeping* magazine while we were perusing for the latest issue of *Tiger Beat.* Thirty years later, she was still baking and decorating cakes for friends' weddings and colleagues' successes and kids' parties, each one fancier and more creative than the next.

Why hadn't I supported her desires the way she'd always supported mine? Why hadn't I ever asked her if she was happy? Why had I only assumed she was? After seeing how elated she was on her wedding day—and she and Bill had gone all out with floral arrangements in crystal vases and champagne fountains and a Viennese dessert table—I'd just assumed that bliss had stayed with her every day since, and that she liked her work because she was good at it and it accommodated her schedule with the kids.

I hugged her. "God, Laurel. I'm so sorry. I didn't know, and I should have."

She accepted my bid. "It's OK. Really."

"Why have you stuck with me all these years?"

"Mostly because I've been waiting for a night like this," she said, playfully elbowing me in the ribs. "But I guess because I've always wanted to be like you. All that talent and success. I kept hoping it might rub off on me. And that I might get brave, too."

"You're the bravest person I know," I said. "In fact, I've always wanted to be like *you*."

Our eyes both misted as we surrendered to the moment.

"Do you still want to be a cake decorator?" I asked.

"More than that. I want to be a party planner."

"It's not too late," I said. "If Taro can make a comeback, then why can't you?"

"At fifty?"

"Why not? You're talented. You're organized. You're great with people. You know how to network. I mean, we wouldn't be here right now were it not for you. So go make your dream come true."

"Do you really think I can?"

"Laurel, you just had dinner with *Taro*. You can do anything."

I really, *really* needed to start listening to my own words.

CHAPTER EIGHTEEN

The ride back to Port Washington was less chatty and animated than things had been on the way to the city—Michael scrolled through his phone, Ian fell asleep, and Laurel stared out the window wearing a contented grin. Meanwhile, I casually conversed with Johnny and Garrett about the tracks we'd laid down two days before, troubleshooting ideas until Laurel chided us to quit talking shop.

"Hey, do you mind if I lay down some additional tracks in your studio and crash at your house for the night?" asked Garrett. "I'm in a working mood."

"Sure," I said. Laurel shot me a not-so-subtle glance, and I nonverbally refuted it.

When the limo pulled into my driveway, each of the guys stepped outside to let Laurel and me out and say goodbye. Laurel and I made the rounds. I embraced and thanked them, one by one, before they piled back into the car. I didn't feel as if I was hugging my colleagues, or clients, or celebrities. I didn't feel as if I was hugging my favorite band. I felt as if I was hugging my friends.

My bandmates.

My team.

Each embrace felt warm. Endearing. Personal.

Garrett lingered and waited for Laurel and me to finish exchanging goodbyes next to her car.

"So what did you wish for?" she asked.

"It's bad luck to reveal one's wishes," I replied coyly.

She looked at Garrett, who patiently waited. "You know he's not here to work, right?"

"What? No, Laurel. It's nothing like that."

"Have you not been paying attention, Joey? Have you not noticed the way he's been looking at you all night?"

I swear to God I hadn't. Maybe because I'd been avoiding looking at *him* all night.

She pensively peered over her shoulder at the limo. "Do you think Ian's wife or Bill would find out if I went back and kissed Ian goodnight on the lips?"

I shot her a warning look. "Laurel."

"I know, I know, OK…" she gave me one final hug, perhaps the best one of all, turned and waved to the guys, and then slid into her car, blasting "Last Call" as she backed out the driveway after the limo pulled away.

Garrett followed me up the walkway. Once inside the house, I closed the door behind us and leaned against it, releasing an exhausted exhale. I kicked off my shoes.

"Well," he said. "That was a lot of fun."

"It was," I said. "Although sometimes I wasn't sure if you were having a good time."

We progressed to the living room and plopped ourselves at opposite ends of the sofa.

"Birthdays aren't really my thing anymore," he said.

"Yours is right around the corner," I said, as if he needed reminding.

He ignored the fact. "It's also been a while since we were all so public like that."

"When was the last time?"

"I honestly can't remember. I was drunk a lot back then. Johnny said it was part of the lifestyle, but really I think we were all just trying to cope. We were kids who saw *A Hard Day's Night* and we thought it'd be so glam to be surrounded and chased by that many fans, but when they climb on your car and bang on the windows, it's bloody claustrophobic and scary. You know what it's like."

"Well, I never had *that* level of fame, but I do remember the claustrophobic feeling of everyone wanting a piece of you. You want so much to be seen, and then when you are, you want so much to be invisible again."

He nodded. "Exactly. Then there's the record company pressuring you for another hit. Do you know they got mad when "Love In, Love Out" came in at number two? It *debuted* at number fucking two on the charts, and you'd think we blew a bloody raspberry."

"Love In, Love Out" was the first single from the album that had followed *Fortune Tellers*. "I didn't know that," I said. "About the single, I mean. I'm sorry."

"Don't get me wrong. It was exciting and fun a lot of the time back then, too. But obviously I wish some things had played out differently."

We were both stuck in the reverie now. "Yeah…" was all I could muster. I stared at him intently. I could almost see the shield protecting his heart. Had it been there even before Gav died, like mine had? I had let mine down for Gav. Would Garrett let his down for anyone? Would I for anyone else?

"Your friend Laurel was very nice," he said, this time with a lilt in his voice. "True blue fan."

"You have to admit, it feels good when people shower you with love and appreciation and attention," I said. "I'm not talking about the crazies, mind you, but the longtime fans who are nothing but gracious and grateful."

"You miss it?"

"Fame? Not really," I said. "Being rushed from city to city and interview to interview and venue to venue, plus the lack of privacy, drove me bonkers. But I loved being on stage and practically getting bowled over by the energy coming back at me."

"You know, Gav *loved* being famous. Every minute of it. He loved the attention, the screaming, the girls throwing their bras on the stage. He even loved the lack of privacy. It was all like a game for him. And he figured when the game got boring or came to an end, he'd simply do something else. It all seemed to roll off his shoulders. He especially loved the parties. He once drank Keith Richards under the table."

That was the Gav I knew. But I also knew the Gav underneath who was lonely. He had confided that to me during one of our phone calls. "There are only two people I'm never lonely with," he'd said. "My brother, and you. But it's even different with you. With Garrett, I'm me. With you, I'm a me that wants to be more. Better."

"You didn't think he had an addiction, too?" I asked Garrett. "You said you were all trying to cope. Don't you think there was something else Gav was trying to deal with?"

Garrett hung his head—whether it was in sadness or

shame, I couldn't be sure. Perhaps both. "We were just doing what good rock-and-rollers are supposed to do. It wasn't until years later, right after the accident…" he trailed off.

Then he seemingly flipped a switch, "You drum just like him, you know. If I didn't know any better, I'd think you were channeling him."

I smiled. "Well, that's the nicest thing anyone's ever said to me."

I couldn't tell if the buzz I was feeling was from the alcohol or the compliment or from the night in general. Garrett smiled back, and for the first time since the night began, his eyes sparkled. He was so handsome, even better-looking than he'd been at twenty, despite the beating his body had taken. That's what a sense of purpose did for you, I think. It made you younger, more attractive. It made you so alive one could feel the prickly tingles that radiated from you. I was awash in tingles; a flash of heat coursed through me and went to my head just like the wine did.

"Can I make a confession?" I asked.

Garrett leaned in slyly, as if others were in the room and he didn't want them to hear me. "Please do."

"I love playing with you—all of you," I quickly added. "I love being part of a band. I always wanted that, and never really got to experience it. Sure, I played with a band when I toured, but the record company didn't want me to be the drummer. It was always a double-edged sword with those A&R guys. Either no one would pay to see a girl drummer that wasn't sexy like Sheila E, front and center, or they wouldn't pay to see a singer that drummed unless you were Phil Collins—and can we please talk about how freaking fantastic Karen Carpenter was at both? She was also one of my idols, even though I don't talk much about her. She made it look so easy, and she never received the credit she deserved—at least not in the mainstream. That's why I ultimately loved being behind the desk in the studio. Everyone finally shut up, you know?"

Garrett examined me. "I never realized what a hard time you had back then."

Self-consciousness washed over me. "I'm babbling," I said. "It was just fame. And pop music. It wasn't anything that really mattered."

"It mattered to *you*."

My eyes misted over. He gestured as if he was about to reach out and put the back of his hand to my cheek but thought better of it, and I was simultaneously relieved and disappointed.

"I hate to be a midlife cliché, but working and playing with you guys these past few months has made me feel twenty years younger."

"Fifty's not so old," he said. "Although you do look younger tonight, with the dress and hair and makeup. You're stunning, really. But even without the makeup you're beautiful. You always were."

I blinked and fell into a momentary trance of puzzlement. What did he mean by *you always were*?

"You said I was a cow," I nearly whispered.

Didn't matter how much weight I lost or makeovers I got. I'd never shed the *feeling* of the word.

He matched my whisper. "I was wrong. In fact, I was a goddamn liar."

Garrett wore an expression of remorse, watching me as I literally squirmed, afraid of his words, his eyes, his lips.

Afraid of the truth.

He slid across the sofa and fully entered my personal space. "I've got a little confession for you, too. Remember that fight in the kitchen when you soaked me with a glass of water?"

"Yessss…"

A net of butterflies let loose inside me.

"Remember I was going to tell you another thing that was hard about making the album?"

"Yessss…"

Forget butterflies. Anxiety swirled in my gut, like the beginnings of a funnel cloud. I did not want to keep going down this road, yet I couldn't seem to stop putting one metaphorical foot in front of the other.

"I was going to tell you that I've never before worked with a producer I was sexually attracted to."

I knew that's what he was going to say. And yet, it still rammed into me like a pack of offensive linemen. It trampled every professional boundary I'd worked so hard to maintain. It defied my frozen-in-time feelings for his twin brother. It cracked the wall I'd built around myself.

I was always going to be a *female* producer as opposed to a producer. There was always going to be the asterisk of "woman" in every accomplishment, every decision, every ounce of talent I gave to every project. I was always going to be objectified first, criticized second, praised in resignation third.

I opened my mouth and I waited for some kind of word, sound, something to come out. Because now I was angry.

"Am I supposed to fall at your feet now?" I spat out. He looked bewildered. "It will never, ever matter how good I am. No musician—no *male* musician—is ever going to look at me as anything other than a potential score. Or a threat."

Garrett straightened his posture and backed away. "That's not what I meant. I'm not trying to be sexist. I'm trying to tell you that I'm attracted to you. To *you*, Johanna."

All night long, he'd called me Johanna, as did the others. The first time anyone other than Aunt Mary Lou had in an incredibly long time. It sounded like a melody coming from his lips.

Johanna. That's who I wanted to be.

My heart began to pulse a steady four-on-the-floor beat. Because *goddammit, I was attracted to him, too. Gavin Chandler's twin brother.* The blunt, rude one who, in the span of thirty-five years, had bedded enough women to populate a city and had sabotaged his own career and... and... did I mention Gavin's twin brother?

Gav was supposed to be my soulmate. Not Garrett.

Soulmates were impossible to live up to. Just like celebrities.

But Garrett was my *friend,* I realized. My best friend. Even more than Laurel. He was the one I wanted to see and talk to and work with every day. A best friend was even better than a soulmate. Equal parts real and magical. Grounding and blissful.

Gav always made me like I was the most special woman in the world. He made me feel cherished. Treasured. Adored.

Garrett made me feel like Johanna. Ordinary—not in the sense of not special or worthy of being cherished or treasured or adored. But more importantly, at home inside myself. *Content.* It was so subtle that I hadn't even noticed it.

"Johanna," he said with tenderness, "I'm trying to tell you that I *feel* something for you."

We sat there, silent and breathless, eyes locked, for a good five seconds. Completely absorbing the truth.

And then, much the way a penned-up bull is released into a rodeo ring, the gate swung open and I unleashed myself, pouncing on Garrett and locking my lips to him in an untamed kiss. He smelled like musk and felt like leather and tasted like cake. He fell back on the sofa and pulled me with him, placing one hand on the small of my back, and running his other up my thigh, then along the contour of my hip and torso to my breast, trying to wedge his fingers inside the lining of the dress and under the cup of my lace bra—all while I kissed him wildly and rustled his shirt, clumsily unbuttoning it, looking for bare chest.

God, it felt more than good. It felt *right.*

Like when we played in the studio. *Chemistry*—the way we interacted, combined, and changed.

And then, as his warm thumb glided over my breast—and my God did *that* feel good, like a lit match that burned without pain—a slideshow of images, memories, and voices bombarded me:

Gav. Beautiful, once-alive Gav, who wanted me forever.

Garrett, my *colleague.*

A future headline: "Producer Tramples Ethics in Favor of Romp with Ex-Teen Heartthrob."

Uncle Oscar, shaking his head in disappointment.

My parents: *We always knew you were no good.*

I hoisted myself up, reflexively pulling my hair back as if to make a ponytail and catching the firmly varnished coif instead, as I tried to catch my breath.

I sprang from the couch and covered my mouth. "Oh my God, what am I doing?"

He sat up. "You're being randy, as you should. He then stood up to approach me. I backed up and headed for the kitchen.

"With *you*?" I said before realizing how insulting it sounded. Thankfully, he laughed.

"Better than Benny, that's for bloody sure."

"No. No no no no. I am your *producer.* I'm a *professional.*"

Garrett turned serious, even beckoning. "There's so much more to you than producer or professional. You're a *woman*, Johanna. An incredibly attractive, passionate woman. Why can't you just leave it at that and enjoy yourself tonight? Really celebrate. You keep telling me to have fun."

"Not *that* kind of fun. You've had plenty of that."

"I mean you should allow yourself the pleasure you deserve."

"You said you wanted to work in the studio tonight."

"I did want to work in the studio."

"You said you were in the mood to *work*."

"I was in the mood to work."

"I thought you meant the *other* work."

"Johanna, this wasn't premeditated."

"Stop calling me that."

"What, your name?"

I focused upon his hair tousled, his shirt unbuttoned, his chest revealed.

He must have seen the lust in my eyes, took note of my mouth open, panting. A wave of emotion crested over me, and tears flooded my eyes.

Solemn and concerned, he asked, "Do you really not want to do this?"

"We *can't* do this."

"Why?"

"You know why."

"Because you're our producer, or because it's me you want to shag right this moment and not my brother?"

And there it was. The raw truth.

It terrified me.

I spied an empty glass on the table, picked it up, and took it to the sink, trying desperately to clear my head.

Garrett followed me. "Johanna ..."

"I told you to stop calling me that."

"Look, I'm sorry for what I said. I'm not trying to be a

git, I'm really not. I'm trying to be honest. I want you. Not because you're a conquest, not because I just want a shag, and certainly not because you're our producer. I want to *be* with you. With *you.* And I don't want you to be afraid of that."

I looked over the sink at the window, which transformed to a mirror at night. I watched Garrett step behind me, his scent piercing me as he touched my arm and made a peace offering rather than a pass. I closed my eyes and sucked in a breath. He took one as well, as if inhaling me, and let it out in a sigh. Its warmth caressed me like a breeze on the back of my neck.

"Please, Joey," he whispered. "I don't want to pressure you. I know you're scared. I am, too, believe it or not, but please trust me. Trust this."

I was a puddle of melted butter.

I closed my eyes and leaned back into him, the way partners do in those trust exercises, allowing him to catch me.

He kissed the spot just under my ear. I moaned with delight as my body surged with caged desire. Moving along my neckline, his mouth, like an instrument, tapped out kisses in rhythm, the beats between the notes.

A silent song. A musical flame.

I turned around, cupped his face, and pulled it to mine for another kiss of surrender. No, of *trust.* And like a scene out of a romance novel or a music video, he swept me into his arms and carried me to my bedroom, his lips never leaving mine.

CHAPTER NINETEEN

I woke up hearing the rhythmic rainfall of the shower spray in the adjoining bathroom, like droplets pattering against a window, and then consciousness—and clarity—interrupted like thunder.

Garrett and me.

Cuddling and spooning and kissing and canoodling.

Orgasms.

Sleep, with a warm body beside me. Sound sleep, in fact.

I had never, *ever* slept with a client. *Especially* while making an album. I wasn't so drunk that I'd lost control of my faculties, so I couldn't blame it on the alcohol.

So why did I do it?

Who was I kidding? I didn't need to ask. I already knew.

Cuddling and spooning and kissing and canoodling.

Could've been a Paisley Parker lyric.

Garrett was tender. He was naked. Not just unclothed, but open. Vulnerable. As was I. It was like being onstage. The surge of energy. The outpouring of aliveness. The *oneness*.

Intimate.

We were Garrett and Johanna last night.

But this morning, we were Taro's Garrett Chandler and Joey Parker, Producer.

I yanked the covers over my head and hid, hoping to reverse the events of the previous twelve hours by process of wishing.

No dice. I poked my nose out before emerging and sitting up, leaning back against the headboard, still naked, when I realized the pattering had ceased. A few minutes later, Garrett emerged, wrapped in a towel and his wet hair slicked back.

The tennis really had done him wonders.

"Morning," he said, chipper. In a sudden bout of modesty, I hoisted the covers up and around me.

"Tell me the truth," I said.

"About what?"

"You said you wanted to work in the studio last night. That's why I let you come over. Because I believed you. And I was actually naïve enough to think that when you had asked to stay over, you were going to crash in the guest bedroom."

"I swear to God, that was my intention, and it was the truth."

"So what happened?"

He cocked an eyebrow, as if to say *isn't it obvious?*

"You have regrets?" His matter-of-factness unnerved me.

"You don't?"

"Not even one."

His certainty unnerved me even more.

"You're lucky I have nothing to throw at your head right

now. I mean, I could hurl this lamp at you, but I like it more than I like you."

He laughed. "Look, if you're worried about babies, don't. I got snipped when I was twenty-one so I wouldn't have to worry about anyone slapping me with a paternity suit. Not to mention that I can't stand kids; sticky little creatures, they are.

"There's also STDs to worry about," I said.

"From you or me?"

I shot him a death glare. "I told you, I don't sleep around. Never did."

"Ever?"

"One time. After a party."

He seemed delighted. "Anyone I know?"

"One of the Brat Pack."

I'd never even told Laurel that.

He crossed his arms and cocked an approving eyebrow. "Which one?"

"Not telling."

He padded to my side of the bed and sat on the edge. "You know, this isn't very good morning-after talk, diseases and keeping secrets and all that."

I recoiled. "Goodbye, Garrett."

Now he was genuinely hurt. "Johanna, seriously. What's going on?"

"You really don't see the problem here?" I asked. "You don't see this for the massive ethical violation it is? We just put the entire project in jeopardy by becoming emotionally, intimately—*sexually* involved. How am I supposed to face you and the others in the studio now? How am I supposed to earn your respect when you're picturing me naked?"

"We all pictured you naked well before last night, Joey. We're blokes, we can't help ourselves."

And I thought we were a family.

"Well, *that* makes me feel better," I said. "Get out, Garrett. Get out of my house. Get out of my studio. Get out of my entire life."

"Johanna, please."

"You take no responsibility whatsoever?"

"Responsibility for what?"

"What was this, anyway? Was it a one-night-only shag? Was it that you had nowhere else to go? Was it a way to emotionally manipulate me?"

"Christ, Johanna. You're the one that doesn't get it."

"What don't I get?"

"If after all this time you think I just wanted to shag you…"

"You all pictured me naked. That's what you just said."

"I was trying to lighten the mood."

"By being a misogynist prick?"

He opened his mouth as if to issue a rebuke, when he closed it and looked out the bedroom window, as if noticing for the first time that the sun was shining.

"You're right," he said softly, in a tone of contrition. "I'm sorry." He compiled the pieces of his suit and hastily reassembled them, then patted down his pockets to make sure his keys and wallet were still in place. "I'll go now."

"It's over, Garrett," I said. "The band, the album. Everything. I can't work with you anymore. I betrayed everything I stand for."

I expected him to lob the ball back with snark, sarcasm, even anger. But he said nothing. Instead, he pulled out his phone, as if he hadn't heard a word I'd said.

"What are you doing?" I asked.

"Calling a car service. I need a ride back to my place. I also need to call the others and tell them we're done."

So he had heard me.

The reality didn't hit me until he said the words: *we're done*. Alarms sirened within me: *May-day, may-day. Don't throw this all away. Take a breath and figure it out.*

"What, you're going tell them about—" I stopped short.

"I won't have to," he said. "They'll know it was me who cocked it up."

"No," I said. "Don't. I'll call them. This is my mess."

He shook his head in exasperation and disbelief, mouthing the word *mess*.

Garrett was clearly wounded. Defeated, even. He stared at me, saying nothing. He was as beautiful as his brother was. The arc of his brows. The curve of his lips. The squareness of his chin.

What if it was supposed to have been him all along?

As he turned to leave the room, I called out: "Garrett, wait."

"I'll see myself out," he said, crestfallen.

And when the front door closed behind him, I burst into tears.

CHAPTER TWENTY

Laurel called me shortly after Garrett left. "Hope you don't mind, but I posted photos of last night on my social media pages. I know I should have asked you first. Fangirl-me fangirls first and thinks second."

"It's fine," I said. My brain felt too weighted down to cogitate beyond that.

"And I told Bill the truth about where we were. He was cool about it, said he kind of already knew."

I didn't respond.

"You OK?" she asked. "Hung over? I didn't think you had that much to drink last night."

I didn't want her to know. Didn't want anyone to know.

And yet, I blurted it out: "I did something stupid last night."

Laurel paused only for a beat before she uttered a baritone "Ohhhhhhh."

"You warned me," I said. "I didn't listen."

"Did he…did he force himself on you?"

"No. I was a very willing participant."

"Then what's the problem?"

"Laurel, would you ever sleep with one of your employees or coworkers? Even if you were single."

"Well, no," she said. "But let's face it, Joey. The music business is no ordinary workplace. I would think the boundaries are a little fuzzy in that regard."

"All the more reason to be vigilant," I replied.

"I think you're being too hard on yourself. After all, you weren't exactly acting alone. What about Garrett?"

"What about Garrett? He got what he wanted."

"And you? Did you get what you wanted? What you needed?"

In the moment, yes. Yes, I did. And it was wonderful. But the moments after that had lasting consequences.

"That's not the point," I said.

"Why not? You're a grown-ass woman who can do what she wants. You wanted him. He wanted you. As long as you both acted on that together, then I don't see the problem. Whose business is it, anyway? Do you really think Michael or Ian or Johnny will care?"

"It's not a matter of caring," I argued. "The project is compromised now. My objectivity is shot. My professional integrity is ruined."

"Joey, YOU GOT LAID. I'm sorry to be so blunt, and I'm sure it meant more to you than that, but that's what it was. Sex. Lovemaking. You weren't selling state secrets."

She was right. So why couldn't I see it that way? Why couldn't I let it roll off my shoulders?

We were both silent for a moment. "Sooooo…" Laurel

tentatively started, and I knew what was about to follow. "How was it?"

"It was real nice," I said sadly. An understatement.

"Joey Parker and Garrett Chandler," she said. "Who could've predicted that?" After a beat, she added. "It was a great party. The best night of my life."

Mine, too.

Later that day, I called Michael, Johnny, and Ian, and told them that the good time we had at my birthday party was proof that we all needed a break, to take a week off and come back refreshed and rejuvenated. Apparently, Garrett hadn't called them yet, and I needed time to decide whether I should step away and let another producer finish up (maybe Nile Rodgers was available?), scrub the entire album, or keep working as if nothing happened. As much as I wanted option three, I knew how unlikely it was that I could look any of them in the eye again.

Then I called Rick. Despite my trying to be casual, he could read my poker face even over the phone. "Did something happen after the party?" he asked.

I met his question with silence. That was all he needed to know.

"Wow," he said.

"I've never put myself in this position before," I said. "You have to know that."

"I do."

"Have I lost your respect?"

"Of course not. You think you're the only one who ever crossed a line?"

"Like this?"

"Exactly like this. This is a business of blurred lines."

Exactly what Laurel said.

"Are you saying you…" I couldn't bring myself to finish.

"Let's just say there are things I hope my wife never finds out about and leave it at that. Except to also say that I, too, felt as you do right now."

"So what did you do about it? What do *I* do?"

"Other than go back to work and do your best to not let it interfere with the job you're doing? Nothing, really."

"You can do it because you're a man. Hell, I'll bet you worked with guys who gave you a pat on the back for it. But they're all going to look at me differently now. They're going to *judge* me."

"Do you really believe that?" he asked.

"I *know* it," I said. "I've been fighting against it my entire career—this goddamn asterisk of my double-x chromosomes. It follows me wherever I go."

A silence lingered for a second. And yet, it spoke a truth: When it came to the music, there were times when Rick and I could practically finish each other's sentences. But we'd never been anywhere near this kind of subject.

Rick came in on the backbeat. "Joey, you're the best producer and engineer I've ever worked with. It took me a long time to figure out what made you so good. It was more than skill or talent. It's your intuition. Your instinct. And I'm not talking about the kind that comes from listening to a lot of records or being in the business since you were old enough to talk. I know it's going to sound sexist the way I say this, but I swear I mean it as the utmost compliment: It's your *woman's* intuition. I don't know how else to say it. You just…you hear more than the music. You hear what's between the notes. You recognize it, identify it with all your senses, harness it, paint a picture and tell a story with sound. You know how to relate and connect better to the magic than anyone I know, in a way I or any other man will never be able to because of our Y chromosomes."

And with that, my friend and colleague Rick made me cry.

"I don't know what to say," I said, my voice breaking on every word.

"You don't have to say anything," he said, equally verklempt. "Just please don't ever see your sex as a liability ever again, OK? I know this business makes you do it, and I'm as guilty as the next guy enabling it. But I want to make it better, starting now."

I could barely utter a thank-you, much less convey the depth of it.

"I have no business telling you what to do next. But selfishly speaking, I'd hate to see all of our work go into the crapper. It's a damn good album, Joey. It's going to be an elixir for everyone who listens to it."

"Thank you," I said. "I'll think about it."

It's not that I didn't believe Rick. It's that I didn't know how to look myself in the eye from here on as Taro's producer. Or anyone else's.

CHAPTER TWENTY-ONE

Michael and Ian flew back to England to be with their families. Johnny went to Los Angeles. I don't know what Garrett did.

As for me, I moped around the house for three days, waffling on the situation. I'd been too hard on Garrett, and I'd hurt him. I wasn't sure if we could get past that, much less the night we spent together. And here I thought our *history* was going to drive a wedge between us. Maybe Rick was right and I just needed to check the baggage at the door when I went to work. Be the professional I am.

Or maybe it was every bit the quagmire I thought it was—that our past was always going to be the wedge—and the project was over, punishment for my poor decision-making.

But had sleeping with Garrett really been a poor decision? Was it really so bad to surrender to my desire as Johanna rather than resist it as Joey Parker? No man in my position would be questioning that. Why did I see it in terms of crime and punishment? Guilt and shame?

And what about Garrett's accountability? Or Taro's? Hadn't we crossed the line the moment we went out to dinner? In fact, hadn't it happened even sooner than that?

Thing is, I *missed* Garrett. I missed his body. His scent. His voice. I missed his touch and his warmth. I missed the music between us.

I missed Taro, too. I missed the work. I missed feeling good about everything.

The longing panged worse than hunger.

On day four, I went downstairs to the studio and laid down some tracks for one of the new songs I'd written over the summer. Drums. Bass. Bare-bones keyboards and acoustic guitar. A scratch vocal.

When the world is behind you
And you don't know the truth
Do you cling to your beauty
Or do you cling to your youth

I barely got the first verse out before bursting into tears.

Day five, I put the finishing touches on the *Been Too Long* remixes.

Day six, I got a haircut. Short. Pixie style. Regretted it the moment I walked out of the salon. Not that it looked bad. Just that I felt like a rebellious teenager declaring: *I'm gonna do what I wanna do and you can't stop me.*

I should've stopped me.

On day seven, Garrett called me. My every muscle contorted like a wet towel being wrung out when I saw the caller ID.

"The others are flying back tomorrow," he said, his words curt, his voice even-keeled and businesslike. "We'll be back to work on Wednesday, probably."

"OK. Thanks for letting me know," I replied. I tried to match his tone, but the quaver was beyond my control.

"You'll be there, too?"

I sucked in a breath and made the decision right then and there. "Yes."

"I don't want to lose the album," he said. "It's all I have left."

Every word a kick in the gut that I deserved.

"I don't want to lose it, either."

A silence passed between us, one full of words that should be communicated and wounds that should be attended to, but weren't.

"OK then. I'll see you soon, Joey."

"Garrett, wait."

"What is it?"

"I want to tell you how sorry I am. I'm sorry I accused you of just wanting to shag me. I'm sorry for the way I reacted and for kicking you out."

The two seconds he took to reply felt like ten minutes. "I understand why you did. But it still hurt."

"You acted so casually about it," I said. "I just assumed—"

"I didn't *act* casual. I was being me. I was feeling good for once in my life."

Tears rolled down my cheeks. "I'm sorry, Garrett, I really am."

"Why does this have to be an either/or for you?" he asked.

Because I'm terrified to lose you, too. Because it's so much easier to be a producer than a lover. Because if you are the truth, then was what I had with your brother a lie I've been living with my entire life?

"It… it just does," I said sheepishly, ashamed of my utter cowardice.

Garrett, no doubt insulted by the copout, ended the call with a defeated, "I'll see you on Wednesday."

CHAPTER TWENTY-TWO

The creative process of making an album can generally go in this order:

1. This is awesome.
2. This is hard.
3. This is shit.
4. I am shit.
5. This might be OK.
6. This is awesome.
7. I am awesome.

Sometimes it's recursive, meaning you may vacillate between 3 and 1 before settling on 5. Or you start on 5, move to 2, and after three all-night sessions and a river of coffee, take it to 6. You don't get to 7 unless the record is a success. But even then you can never get around or fully escape from 4. Only varying degrees of it.

At the moment, I was feeling hardcore 4.

I drove to East Hampton playing out every version of how the session could go—from smooth sailing to crashing on the rocks and splitting into smithereens. From business-as-usual to awkward-plus-infinity. I was confident that I'd be able to face Rick with my head held high. With Johnny, Ian, and Michael, if not held high, then at least not sunk into my feet.

Garrett, of course, was the X-factor. I didn't know what to expect from him. Or me. Would I dissolve into a puddle on sight? Would he forgive me? Could we move on?

Using my key, I entered Garrett's house and announced my presence. As I entered the makeshift recording studio—as if I were walking the plank—my heart thumped like a bass drum, full and fat and loud enough to shake the walls.

"You cut your hair!" exclaimed Ian the moment he saw me.

"Yes," I said. "Yes, I did."

"Don't tell me you're already having a midlife crisis, Joey," said Ian. "You've got another five years for that."

"What made you do it?" asked Johnny.

"I was tired of you all being cuter than me," I said.

Johnny laughed. Ian, with a playful scoff, said, "No one will ever be cuter than us."

Garrett, whom I could barely look at, took note as well. "It's quite stylish," he said. They were the first words he'd said since I entered the room, and the first time we made eye contact. Like two people trying to touch each other with a see-through partition between them. Each putting their hand to their side of the glass, desperately longing to feel flesh rather than flatness.

And yet, Garrett's opinion still mattered the most to me.

"Thank you," I said, hoping the words didn't sound as stilted as they felt.

Could the others sense the tension? Could they see the pains we were taking to pretend everything was normal? Could Garrett recognize that, despite everything, I still wanted him? Did he still want me?

I wanted to be in his arms. To tell him I was sorry. To do it all over again. To never have done it in the first place.

The break seemed to have done the band some good—Michael, Ian, and Johnny were visibly refreshed. Clean-shaven and dressed in new clothes with brighter colors. They were relaxed amid the gaggle of gear and cables and couches, coffee cups by their side, smiling and jamming. I wished I'd taken a snapshot, or perhaps even video, just to preserve the moment for myself. The metallic smell of equipment mixed with the aroma of coffee and bacon, egg, and cheese bagel sandwiches, the sound of fingers on frets, the sight of dabbling melodies and friendly invention, like kids playing tag, nearly knocked me over with its overwhelming validation.

God, I how love this. How I love *them.*

I would miss this. I *already* missed this.

This was my happy place. These were my people. I knew this world inside and out and couldn't imagine being anywhere else. An office job, a master's degree, a car full of soccer kids might as well be life on Mars. It made 3 and 4 on the list bearable, even worthwhile.

But still unavoidable.

"Well," I said following a deep breath. "Let's get to work."

Taking a break from listening to the tracks had also done some good. We returned to them with a fresher ear and felt better about them now than we had a week ago. We were bobbing our heads as we listened, which was always a good sign.

This might be OK.

It was time to make decisions about which songs to toss

and which to keep for the album, and what order to put them in. An album tells a story. It may not be a literal one, but each song contributes to an overall sound picture. Perhaps the pun had been intentional, but I had always thought the *Pet Sounds* cover with the Beach Boys at a petting zoo was a stupid marketing ploy. The phrase "pet sounds" referred to Brian Wilson's favorite sounds—bells and tick-tocks and melatrons, to name a few. INXS's *Kick* is another example of an album that is so cohesive that the whole is greater than the sum of its parts. Every song on that album works together, like links in a chain. Listen to the defining albums of each decade—The Beatles' *Sgt. Pepper's Lonely Heart's Club Band*, Carole King's *Tapestry*, Michael Jackson's *Thriller*, Nirvana's *Nevermind*, Amy Winehouse's *Back to Black*—and you'll hear it. Like a five-course meal—each course, although distinct, contributes to the overall taste experience. The flavors complement one another. The presentation entices us. And all good cooks know that the secret ingredient is love.

Ditto for music.

Fortune Tellers was one of those albums. Certainly, I'd wanted *Next Wave* and all my other albums to be among them.

Taro wanted to release the album on vinyl in addition to digital and CD, and voted to include no more than ten songs, plus B-sides for singles. Yet we knew the executives would want bonus tracks for the CD and digital downloads. We debated on whether even ten was too many, given the current culture of music consumption that consisted of downloading songs buffet style rather than listening to albums straight through. We all longed for the days when albums in their entirety were something to be savored rather than serving as one of many distractions. They used to be the soundtracks of our lives rather than the sponsorship of our goods. They were storybooks in sound. Paintings in pitch. Fans felt a sense of ownership rather than entitlement. Albums were a part of our DNA.

"Seeing as how vinyl has made a full comeback, we should push that medium hardest," Garrett suggested. "In fact, that should be the album's title. *Come Back.* Two words. That could also be the first single, since we've already got the track. It's one of the stronger ones, too."

The band agreed, as did I.

The goal, then, was to find those ten songs that best made the whole greater than the sum of its parts. That would make modern consumers defy their cultural habits and purchase the full album, sit back, and actively *listen.* Start to finish. Side One and Side Two. No other distractions. Let the story unfold.

Sometimes you don't know what the story is until you listen to what you've got. The title *Come Back* was a good start. We were noticing repeated themes of it in many of Ian's lyrics—then and now, old and new, reinvention. Come back better than before without forgetting who you were. Come back from where you were without losing sight of where you are.

"I love it," I said.

When we stopped for an early dinner, Michael pulled me into one of the other rooms.

"What's going on with you and Garrett?" he asked.

Every muscle knotted as I once again tried to be casual. "What do you mean?"

Garrett and I had been going out of our way to avoid conflict, backing each other up and perhaps being too agreeable.

Michael inhaled, and then blurted it out. "OK. I'm just going to say it. I know it's none of my business—well, technically it is my business given that we're making an album together, but—"

So much for being casual. I put up a hand to halt the lecture that Michael was about to deliver.

"Don't," I said. "It's *not* your business, album or not, and it's not up for discussion. It's between me and Garrett."

"Fair enough," he said. "Just know that we're all aware of the elephant in the room."

I wanted to punch a wall as guilt and shame and anger pushed to the surface. "Did he tell you?"

"He didn't have to."

And that was when I realized that I just did. *Shit.*

I folded my arms across my chest. "Then why are we talking about this?"

"Joey, I'm sorry. I just…we're so close."

"You think I don't know that?" I said, trying to keep my voice down.

"We can't finish it without you."

"I have no intention of letting you down."

"I know that."

"Then I repeat: Why are we talking about this?"

"Well, isn't this cozy," said Garrett, before Michael could reply. My neck practically snapped as it followed the direction of his voice. He peered at Michael. "Shall I snap a photo to send to the wifey?"

"Stop being a petty wanker, Garrett," said Michael. "This is all your fault, you know."

"*My* fault? What did she tell you? Are we about to play He-Said-She-Said? Shall I file a sexual harassment claim like a good office boy?"

Before I had a chance to react, Michael shoved Garrett. Garrett lunged to shove back when, without thinking, I wedged myself between the two of them and he knocked the both of us over.

"You're an awful human being!" hollered Michael. "You blame everyone for your faults. Take responsibility for once in your life."

"You have no idea," Garrett hollered back. "You have no idea how much fucking responsibility I've taken!"

He shook as he yelled. Still on the floor, I looked up at him, towering over us, and saw something frantic in his eyes, as if he were teetering on the edge of a cliff.

"Both of you stop it!" I yelled. "We are *not* doing this."

Garrett extended a hand and pulled me up. I smoothed myself out, just as pain pinched my lower back. I turned to Michael and forwarded the extension.

I repeated, "We are not doing this. Everything was fine until you opened your mouth, Michael." I then whipped around to Garrett. "And once again, you are making everything worse, so cut the crap. It's everyone's fault, and it's no one's fault."

Garrett's eyes turned fiery, and for a moment I thought he was going to hit me. He then stormed back to where the others were and thundered, "EVERYBODY OUT. This album is *over.*"

Johnny rolled his eyeballs. "Now what?"

"This isn't me being histrionic. This is me telling you to *get the fuck out of my house*. We're done."

"Not until we get an explanation," said Ian.

"I never should have let you talk me into this. Do you see what's happened? She's totally taken over. She's taken over our sound and our identity. She's screwed with our heads," he said, pointing his index finger at his temple and making a twirling motion.

"*She* has a name," said Rick. "Show Joey the respect she deserves."

"Johanna," I corrected. Everyone turned their heads to me. Even I was shocked.

Ian looked at Garrett. "Are you high? Seriously, have you fallen off the wagon? Because you're gibbering like you're mad."

"Out of my house," repeated Garrett. "I'm tired of being the target of everyone's wrath. You want to make this album? Then make it without me. But good luck, because you'll have to start over and write your own fucking songs and call it something else because I'll sue you if you use anything with Taro's or my name on it. And all that crowdsourcing money? Down the loo."

"Do you realize what you're saying? What you're *doing*?" I said. "You're throwing away months of blood, sweat, and tears because you're mad at me. Fire me if you must, but please don't throw it all away."

"*You're* the one who said it was over, you hypocrite," said Garrett to me with a heart-piercing glower.

"No one's getting fired," said Michael.

"Think of the fans," I said. "Like Laurel. They're going to be so incredibly let down, and you'll lose them for good."

"If you don't all get out of my house in the next sixty seconds, I'll fucking move," said Garrett.

"Garrett, this is ridiculous," said Johnny. "We're all mates here. Let's work it out."

"Please," I added.

"Stop acting like you know us," said Garrett to me. "You know *nothing*."

What did he mean by *us*? Taro? Him and Gav? Him and me?

"She does know us," said Michael. "That's the fucking problem, isn't it? She knows everything."

"*You* don't even know everything," said Garrett to Michael. "None of you do. Now. Get out."

After ten seconds of a silent standoff, I conceded. "Guys, let's pack up."

This is shit.

We are shit.

CHAPTER TWENTY-THREE

Johnny, Ian, Michael, Rick, and I convened at a coffee shop in Southampton, crowded around tables pushed together. Johnny, Michael, and Ian wore hats and shades to hide their faces, which only made them more recognizable, of course.

"This is all my fault," I said.

"None of this is your fault," said Michael. "Garrett's always been difficult, but never this volatile."

"He's a powder keg, and he finally blew," Johnny said.

"Wouldn't you be, too, had your twin brother died so young?" I said. "I mean, think about that. Your *identical* twin brother. You all knew him, of course, but imagine knowing him before you were even born. Being born together."

They all stared blankly at the table.

"So what do we do now?" asked Michael, dejected.

"Let him cool off," Ian said. "He always does."

"Not this time," said Johnny. "You heard him. He's in no space to accept anything we or anyone else has to say."

A second somber silence followed.

"I am not letting him ruin this for us" Ian said. "Not again. Never again. Janet said Sony wants to hear what we've got. The fan community has been recharged. I will not let him destroy it."

"Maybe we can talk to him in a day or two," Michael offered.

"Don't try to save him," warned Johnny. "You can't. The only one who can save Garrett is Garrett."

"I guess we're on holiday again," said Ian. "Bloody hell. First time I don't want to be."

Ian followed through on his threat—or promise—and sent the album to Taro's management, who loved it and forwarded it to Sony, who also loved it and were ready to officially offer Taro a contract.

Would there be enough to finish it as-is, without Garrett? Would Garrett sign the contract but opt out of touring? Would he actually sue to block the others from signing?

Regardless, the fate of the album was perilous, at best. At worst, dead in its tracks, as was Taro itself. There would be no other chance for a comeback after this. They'd used up all their lifelines.

As for me, I could already envision a new headline: "Joey 'Paisley' Parker Ruins Taro, Quits the Music Business in Disgrace." Not to mention the possible legal ramifications of not fulfilling my contractual obligations to produce the album.

Turned out I'd gotten what I'd wanted: I was done with the

music business. Or rather, the music business was done with me. Had I been pushed off the cliff, or had I willingly jumped? And would the chute open or would I plummet to my demise?

One week later, around midnight, my phone rattled me awake. I reached for it and saw Garrett's name and number on the caller ID.

This can't be good.

After a tentative hello from me, Garrett's spoke: "Joey, could you come here, please? I fucked up. I really, really fucked up and I don't know who else to call."

He was crying. He was also drunk.

CHAPTER TWENTY-FOUR

I swung my legs over the edge of the bed to sit up. "What happened?" I asked.

"Please," he sobbed.

I was out of bed and already hurriedly dressing while I replied, "I'm on my way and I'll be there as soon as I can. You know it's going to be a couple of hours. Garrett, I'm going to keep you on the phone the entire time, OK?"

"OK." He whimpered like a child.

I finished dressing, then grabbed my keys and wallet. I peeled out of the driveway and sped seventy-five miles per hour east on the Long Island Expressway, vigilant for police cars with radar guns, talking to Garrett about anything I could think of: The weather. Favorite books. TV shows. Albums. Soccer team. Best drum sound. Guitar solo. Concert venue. Tennis player. Who was better at Live Aid: Freddie Mercury and Queen or Mick Jagger and Tina Turner. Were you to ask me to recall a single answer from either of us, I couldn't tell you, for I was also trying to stave off the mental images of what I might find when I arrived, especially if I was too late.

I pulled into the driveway around two forty-five a.m. after punching in the security gate code. At the door, I flipped my ring of keys until the one to his door appeared, and let myself in, hoping the alarm wasn't set.

Darkness, except for the light from my phone.

Eerie silence, except for my calling his name.

No answer.

Had he been somewhere else when he called and didn't mention it? On the beach, maybe? I'd ended the call the moment I arrived and announced I was there, not thinking to ask which room he was in.

I foraged through the house until I saw a dim light emanating from the TV room, then I raced there. When I reached the entrance, I took in the horror:

Empty vodka bottles. Empty pizza boxes. Throw pillows on the floor. A shattered TV screen and a smashed remote control among the rubble.

I gasped. *Holy shit.*

Garrett was slouched on the floor, his back against the couch, legs spread in a V, a half-consumed bottle of Absolut in hand. His face was tear-streaked, and he hadn't showered in days. I covered my mouth and suppressed a gag as tears stung my eyes, then I quickly composed myself.

I forced out a calm, casual greeting. "Hey."

He slowly turned his head but didn't reply.

"What's going on?" I wasn't sure if acting as if I was there to shoot the breeze rather than crisis management was the right approach, but I seemed to be on autopilot.

Finally, he spoke. "Yesterday was Gav's birthday. *Our* birthday."

I put my hand to my open mouth as my eyes welled.

"Oh my God, Garrett. I completely forgot."

I had *never* forgotten Gav's and Garrett's birthday.

When we were kids, Laurel and I marked each Taro birthday on the calendar with colorful pens. We celebrated them with marathons of Taro videos, donning a T-shirt featuring the birthday boy's face, making their favorite foods (according to the teen magazines), and cupcakes we baked and ate on their behalf after we sang happy birthday (I even did harmony vocals). For the twins' birthday, Laurel would wear the Garrett tee and I would wear the Gav tee.

And of course, we'd make up stories about how we'd meet them and become their girlfriends. I had loved that Gav's and my birthdays were so close, even though we were four years apart. I had fantasized that Gav and I would have double celebrations. With Garrett, of course. There would be no leaving out the twin.

That had been the only time I was like every other teenage girl, one who wasn't obsessed with listening to records to learn technique as opposed to enjoying them. Sometimes I wished the teen fantasy had stayed intact. At least my heart had never been broken in the fantasy.

And he would have still been alive.

Gavin Chandler. My soulmate. He would've been fifty-four.

Garrett Chandler. My lover. He *was* fifty-four.

How in the world had I forgotten? How had I lost the day?

Because I had been so self-absorbed, so consumed with how all that had transpired had affected *me* that I'd barely looked at a calendar.

The guilt sat on my chest, threatening to crush me.

"I somehow managed to get through this past decade of birthdays sober," said Garrett. He sounded exhausted yet still slurred his words. "But I couldn't do it this time."

I sat beside him and took the bottle from his hands, wishing I'd picked up a couple of coffees from a 7-Eleven on the way.

"What made it so difficult this time?" I asked as I tucked the bottle behind me, out of sight.

He turned to face me again. "You." His tears resumed. "I have to tell you something. The others don't even know this."

He cupped his hand to his lips, discovered that the bottle wasn't in it, and scowled.

"The night of the accident, Gav told me that he was going to marry you. Said he was sure of it. I told him it was a load of rubbish, that he'd been drinking too much and didn't know what he was saying. But the truth is, I was jealous."

I sat on my knees, stymied, my brain and heart on delayed reaction, failing to understand. "Jealous of what?"

"I don't know. Him settling down? Potentially breaking up the band and leaving the music business? Finding someone before I did? Not being in competition with me for getting the most girls anymore?" He paused for a couple of beats before confessing, "Or maybe it was because I loved you myself."

You know the feeling when you witness something so shocking it takes you a moment to fully digest it, like it's happening in slow motion? The stark truth of Garrett's confession was taking its time to fully sink in.

"But...you..."

"I know. I called you a cow. Said a lot of really mean things to and about you. It's what I do, even if I don't remember doing it. Whenever I feel insecure about something, I cover it up by being an asshole. It was how I coped with being bullied as a kid. Did you know that?"

I shook my head.

"We were small for our age. And wore glasses. And dressed the same."

I flashed back to my own childhood. I got made fun of for wearing Wrangler jeans when everyone was wearing Jordache.

Garrett was someplace else. His English hometown in the early 1970s, I guessed.

"Gav never let bullies get to him—I don't know how he did it, but he simply didn't believe a word they said. And besides, people just naturally liked him. I had enemies. Gav had friends he hadn't made yet. Even the bullies eventually got around to liking him. And maybe I hated him for that too. As close as we were, we were also fierce rivals. We competed on everything—who had more toy soldiers, who was the better tennis player, who could write a better song...Gav won every time. He was even born first. By three minutes."

Garrett wiped his nose with the end of his shirt, sniffled, and fast-forwarded the timeline. "That night..." He choked up and began to cry again. I inched closer and took his hand into mine. "After you left, we got into a huge row. He told me he was going to propose to you—'for the rest of our lives,' he said—and I wouldn't let him. He even alluded to leaving the band. That's when I lost it. I said all kinds of nasty things, and he was furious with me. We'd both drank a lot, and I told him to sod off. And then I gave him the keys to the car."

He erupted in a wail. *"I GAVE HIM THE KEYS."*

I yanked my hand from his—in an instant, a screen appeared before my mind's eye, showing me a reel of the scene. Garrett and Gavin, identical, yet in opposition to each other. The confrontation. Slurred speech. Insults exchanged. Voices raised. And then, in slow motion, *the moment*: Car keys, passed from hand to hand. Not a torch or a baton, but keys to death's door. And with each screenshot, the horror dug in deeper.

Garrett cried. "He stomped out of there and I knew he was driving blitzed." He collapsed into me and buried his face into my shoulder. "I let him get in that car and drive. I even told him to run himself off the road!"

Tears cascaded down my cheeks as I was bombarded by all the what-ifs and if-onlys that had been stolen from me. A lifetime of kisses. Of lovemaking. Of a future. Of *music.*

He sobbed. "I forget so much when I'm drunk. Why couldn't I forget that?"

My stomach churned while my mind raced—betrayed, bereaved, befuddled. *How could you?* I wanted to scream. *How could you do that to your twin brother? To all of us?*

You'd think Garrett had just read my mind. "Say you hate me," he said as he sat upright again. "I've been trying to make you hate me all this time."

I clenched my teeth. "You almost succeeded." And then, perhaps to protect my heart, I made it about business. "How could you go all these months—all these *years*—without telling me this? Did you think working with me would somehow make amends?"

He shook his head. "No, that wasn't it. I didn't want to work with you, didn't trust myself around you and the others. But I finally admitted to myself that I really wanted to make the album. And you were the right person for the job. You were the *only* person for the job. The band knew it. I knew it. I thought I could...I don't know, I thought I could work around the truth somehow. First, I tried pushing you away. But I liked being your friend."

I liked being your friend, too.

"And when we played together—I've never felt that

connection with anyone but Gav, like playing with your soulmate or something."

Like playing with your soulmate.

"And it both tortured and elated me. And then, when we… I'm sorry you got the impression that I treated you like you just another shag. But you make me feel vulnerable in every way."

My brain was swimming. "I don't understand," I said. "What do you mean?"

"We're good collaborators is what I'm trying to say. I never collaborated with anyone but Gav and the band. I never even played tennis with anyone but him. What scared me the most was that it was *better* than with him because I wasn't in competition with you. And probably none of it would've happened had he still been alive and married to you."

"How do you know it wouldn't?" I cried. "We never got the chance. None of us got the chance."

He sobbed. "I've wanted to switch places with him ever since. Give him back to you, back to the world, and put myself six feet under."

I tried to shake off the wooziness that had set in. I felt like the rope in a tug-of-war, afraid my body would literally rip apart at any moment. *God, how can I hate him and love him at the same time?* I was angry and afraid and compassionate and understanding.

No, not afraid. *Vulnerable.* That's what I was feeling. He made me feel vulnerable, too.

He purged yet another confession. "While you were dealing with the guilt of having compromised your ethics, I was dealing with the guilt of having been with the woman who my brother and best friend loved, and who loved him. Back then, I was arrogant enough that I might have literally fought him for you. But the night of your birthday, I thought maybe…maybe now he was giving me his blessing. At first, I was OK with it and I was being completely honest when I told you I had no regrets. And I swear, Joey—I wanted to work in the studio that night. I thought it would help me dispel my feelings. But in the days that followed, it haunted me. You were his. You should have always been his."

I was drained. Exhausted. Depleted. Torn wide open.

"I wasn't a prize to be won," I said.

"Johanna, from the moment you entered my world, I never saw you as a prize. You have to believe me."

"I don't know how."

"I don't want to lose you," he said. "I know I've pushed everyone in my life away, but I now know how much I need them. And you. Especially you. I'm most afraid to lose you."

Every word a candle of truth shedding light in all the dark places—of our past, our present, even our future.

I didn't belong to anyone. My parents never wanted me. Uncle Oscar and Aunt Mary Lou took me in and loved me as their own, but I wasn't. Hell, *I* hadn't even belonged to me. The record company tried to own me, and when I gave up on Paisley Parker, so did the rest of the world.

I spent fifty years on an island.

I chased a desire to play the drums and learned to keep the beat. I chased a dream of becoming a pop star, and I even roped it, until that rope somehow lassoed itself around me. I chased a profession while trying to outrun my gender. I chased a fantasy of love, and it died at the hand of a bottle and a brother.

I hadn't even realized that all that chasing was actually escape attempts: *Johanna Parker isn't good enough as she is.*

For the first time in my life, I realized that perceived truth had actually been a lie.

And Garrett Chandler lived all these years with that same

lie: That he wasn't good enough. That he wasn't worthy.

I cried. Hard. Garrett and I leaned into each other, my head on his shoulder, his head balanced on mine. We cried together.

Tears of anger.

Of regret.

Of pain.

Of understanding.

Of forgiveness.

When we had finally expended every emotion, we pulled apart. I dried my eyes and blew my nose. Took a few deep breaths. We sat in silence, until I looked at him as a thought came to me.

"How have you coped all this time sober?"

I didn't mean for the question to be condescending or judgmental. I was genuinely curious. How would I have coped?

He shrugged. "I go to meetings. I call my sponsor. I do everything I'm supposed to do. Everything but go to therapy. I thought music was the therapy. Music, it turns out, was the reminder."

"When did you relapse?"

"Day before yesterday."

All this carnage in forty-eight hours.

"Why didn't you call your sponsor?"

"Because I needed to come clean to *you*. I needed to finally take responsibility, just like Michael said."

"I think you need to come clean to them, too. Michael and Johnny and Ian loved your brother as much as you and I did. Maybe not the same way, but they did. Still do. You owe them as much as you owe me."

His face crumpled as he sobbed again. "I can't. I can't lose their love and respect, too."

"But don't you see how much love and respect you've

already taken from them? By refusing to keep the band together, by being so difficult to work with, by lying to them day in and day out. You can't have it both ways anymore, Garrett. You either let them in or keep them out. You either love them and risk losing them, or you lie to them and hate yourself for the rest of your life."

"My fate is already sealed on hating myself."

"It doesn't have to be. You can forgive yourself. You may have given the keys to Gav, but he took them. He got in the car."

Our eyes met, mystified, as that realization came to full fruition for the both of us. More than that, it was like a code that unlocked the cage we'd been living in.

"Everyone who saw him leave that night and knew he was drunk—including Gav himself—shares a piece of that responsibility. It's not all on you," I said.

"I'm the one who made him mad enough to leave."

"Garrett, if you spend the rest of your life hating yourself, then you'll never be able to accept the love others have for you, and you'll never be able to give it. And that is a horrible way to live. You may think that's the punishment you deserve, but if your wombmate were here right now, he'd tell you how wrong you are. So many people love you and want your love."

Good advice. Maybe I should take it.

He stared at his feet. "I don't deserve anyone's love," he finally said above a whisper.

I understood that feeling as well, I realized. It was something Gav had never felt, would have never comprehended.

Garrett and I sat in solidarity, rocking each other. And then, a voice inside me—was it mine? Gav's? Uncle Oscar's?—said with all the clarity and resolve of an actual voice: *Enough.*

It was time to stop with *shoulda, woulda, coulda.* It was time to stop with *if only*. It was time to stop trying to escape something that was always going to be a part of me, of Garrett, of *us*. It was time to stop searching through the wreckage for something to salvage. Time to invent something completely new.

Like an album. One that tells a new story.

Not because Gav would have wanted it this way, or Uncle Oscar, or anyone else. But because *I* wanted it.

It was time to live—not for them, but for me.

I could have a different life and not lose who I am. A blank canvas wasn't about throwing out the old one, rendering it meaningless. It was about creating something repurposed, and that something could be exciting yet still original.

And I didn't have to do it all by myself.

I stood up, and extended my hand. "Get up," I said.

Garrett, his eyes red and glassy and tired, looked at me, dazed. Then he took my hand and heaved himself up, stumbling as he tried to steady himself and falling onto the sofa, knocked over by a wave of dizziness. I helped him to his feet again, placed his arm around my shoulder, and walked him into one of the guest bedrooms on the main floor. It still smelled like Ian.

Maybe you should shower first, I thought as I caught a foul whiff.

Garrett collapsed onto the bed and sidled to one of the pillows, pulling it to him and hugging it with one final sob.

"Get some sleep," I said. I'm not sure he even heard me or felt the kiss I pressed to his forehead as I stroked his hair. "Happy birthday."

I then went to my designated room and crawled under the bedcovers, hugging the pillow just like Garrett and falling asleep within seconds.

CHAPTER TWENTY-FIVE

I awoke around eleven a.m. and searched Garrett's entire house for hidden liquor bottles after I disposed of empty or remaining ones. The cleaning service would be in for a shock when they saw the condition of some of the rooms. They'd been earning their money ever since the band and I set up shop here, but the past few days had turned the place more into the aftermath of a frat party.

Garrett slept past noon.

He didn't look much better than the night before, even after he took a shower—was a little green around the gills and unshaven, and he wore sunglasses indoors. I went out on a coffee and bagels run and came back armed with plenty of both. The bread especially helped settle his stomach.

He groaned. "I don't remember ever feeling this awful, and believe me, I've been on some benders in my life."

"Your body can't handle it anymore," I said. "You're no longer used to it."

"I just want you to know that I'm recommitted. I don't want to do it again."

I believed him. "Do you remember what we talked about last night?"

He nodded slowly. "I remember most of it. I know what I told you."

"Will you go to an AA meeting today?"

"I already called my sponsor and asked him to pick me up. He'll be here in an hour. Listen, Joey..." he started. "Johanna. I can't thank you enough for being here with me. You didn't have to, especially after the way I treated you the last time we were all here. I'm sure my apologies seem empty now, but I am sorry."

Garrett was right—to some extent, his apologies had become empty, trite, just short of disingenuous. What would he say the next time one of us pushed his insecurity buttons, regardless of whether the intention to do so was deliberate? It would inevitably happen again.

But last night was different. Last night was hitting bottom. It was surrender. We've all been there, in one form or another. And when we were in that place, we were all deserving of forgiveness, of a second chance. It didn't matter how many second chances had come before that. The slate wiped clean every time.

"You're welcome," I said.

"I have no right to ask this of you, but will you stay here with me this week? I want to go back to the band and finish the album—if they'll have me back—but I'm not ready yet. I just need a little more time to be sober and work the program again. I don't want to be here alone, though.

I took in a breath.

"I..." I didn't know what to say next.

"I know I'm asking you to cross yet another boundary," he said. "Thing is, I'm not asking you from musician to producer. I'm asking you as a friend."

The word *friend* weighed even heavier than the word *producer* and seemed to be even more demanding. I believed myself to be far more skilled, confident, and familiar with the latter than the former.

But being a friend, I'd come to realize, generated more intrinsic rewards than being a producer. Being a friend also had a longer shelf life. Maybe leaving the music business meant that I could cultivate more friendships, and fine-tune the ones I already had, starting with Laurel.

And Taro.

"I'll stay today and tomorrow," I said. "After that I'll decide on a day-by-day basis. Is that a fair compromise?"

I saw him smile for the first time, and his color returned. "It is. Thank you."

While Garrett went to his meeting, I went into town to pick up some essentials—food, paper products, clothing, and laundry detergent—and attempted to make something healthy for dinner. I put together a salad and grilled chicken breasts with a mustard glaze thanks to a recipe I found online. Garrett took a few bites of each and promised to make a hearty sandwich with the leftovers the following day, which he did.

I decided to stay for the rest of the week.

Two days later, the dark circles around Garrett's eyes disappeared. He was clean-shaven again, and he got a haircut. He even asked the stylist to cover the gray. He went to AA meetings with his sponsor. When I learned the forecast called for heavy rain the next couple of days, I went into town yet again to pick up a few more things I needed. On impulse, I bought a jigsaw puzzle as well. The *Sgt. Pepper's Lonely Hearts Club Band* album cover. One thousand pieces.

"Thought we could do this in lieu of tennis since we're rained out," I said. "Not quite a muscular workout, but good brain activity."

Garrett grinned when he saw it. "I haven't done one of these since we were kids."

"Let me guess: You and Gav competed to see who could fit the most pieces together."

"That, and who wound up with the final piece. One time we got to the end and discovered there was a piece missing from the box. We would leave the finished puzzle out for days before taking it all apart. I didn't see the point in doing so with a missing piece, but Gav insisted. Turned out the little bugger hid it in his pocket and fit it in later, just so he could get the last one."

I laughed out loud. "And here I thought you were the nasty brother."

He laughed as well. "You have no idea, Miss Johanna." He stopped and stared into nothingness for a second before returning to me. "It's nice to talk about him this way without feeling like I'm being set on fire, but the sadness never leaves. I wish it would. It's like a bitter aftertaste you can't quite wash away."

"Lord knows you've tried."

His expression became inquisitive. "Do you have any family, Joey? I've never heard you mention anyone."

My throat tightened. "Not really," I said. "I mean, not anymore. I have an aunt in Florida that I'm close to. I was especially close to her husband, my dad's brother, when I was younger, but he had a heart attack and died around the same time Gav did. I severed my relationship with my parents when I turned eighteen. They're still alive, but I don't talk to them."

He reached out and tucked my hair behind my ear, then rested his warm hand on my cheek. "I'm sorry," he said, caring and earnest. "I'm so sorry you've been alone for so long."

The truth of his words opened my chest like a sinkhole that I thought I might fall into. And then I realized: Maybe that's a good thing. When you finally give pain the oxygen it needs, it burns itself out.

We worked on the puzzle for hours, feeling like kids staying home from school on a snow day. The rain poured in sheets, and we watched as it beaded down the floor-to-ceiling windows in the piano room. Despite the matching charcoal sky and ocean, the view looked like art and sounded melodic.

"We should record that sound," I said.

Garrett caught me spying the microphones on the other side of the room. "Let's try," he said. He moved two mics to the window and together we positioned them, connecting them to an amplifier that routed to the computer. We then opened Pro Tools.

"Please don't stop," I beckoned to the weather gods.

I instructed Garrett to hit record and we ran the program for sixty seconds. Then I looped the audio, adjusting it with the faders and EQ. "Let's do another one," I said, after slightly repositioning the mics. Getting the right sound required delicate touches as opposed to heavy-handedness. We recorded another sixty seconds. We did it three more times, making subtle adjustments with both the mics and the faders until we got the sound I wanted, and just as the rain began to let up.

"Brilliant," said Garrett. "I don't think I would have thought to do that."

"You mean add the reverb?"

"I mean record the sound in the first place. Or maybe I would've thought about it but I wouldn't have followed through."

I smiled. "This is why I'm me and you're you."

He smiled back. "Gav would have. He was into all that shit. I mean that in a nice way."

After we returned the mics to their original places, Garrett said, "I've been meaning to show you something." Joining me at the mixing desk and the computer, he surfed with the mouse, clicking on files until he found what he wanted.

"It's the multi-track files to *Fortune Tellers*," he said. "Figured you'd like to take them out for a spin."

My eyes grew wide, like a kid who's just been handed the world's last candy bar. "Do. Not. Tease. Me."

He looked happy to be the giver of this musical chocolate. "See and hear for yourself." He punched up the first song. "Raindance" poured through the speakers, and I was in my happy place as I shrieked with delight. Immediately, I played with the faders just as I had done with *Been Too Long*, isolating tracks, adding and subtracting in gradations, fiddling with Gav's drum track and giggling all the while. We sat there for two hours as I did this with every song. Garrett even exclaimed, "Blimey, I think you actually improved the mix on that one. Edgar would be angry!"

"That's sacrilege talk right there," I said. "You know Edgar is the reason I took such an interest in engineering." I had told him that, hadn't I?

"It shows. Yet another reason why you and my brother were peas in a pod. I was all about the writing and playing and the process. He was all about the *sound*. It was like I was the writer and he was the editor, know what I mean? I told the story, and he made it readable."

"You complemented each other well in that aspect."

In an instant, the light left his eyes, and I could actually feel the spark snuffed from my own. A morose cloud covered us as we stared into a distant yesteryear. "It hurts, doesn't it?" I said.

"Every day. It's like living without a part of yourself. An arm or a leg, or being blind or deaf. I've never felt whole since."

"I just can't imagine."

"You can, though, Johanna," he said. "I've been listening to your songs, you know. You write about being lost in this world. You write about looking for what makes you whole."

The revelation that Garrett had been listening to my music, and that he'd touched on something so deep, blew through me like a fierce wind; I shivered as if I was naked and defenseless.

And yet, he'd already seen me naked.

Our eyes connected, and in them reflected pain and sympathy and searching and longing and understanding and healing and death and life and love and music. Always music. But like so many times with Garrett, I was also seeing between the notes—I was never some empty vessel needing to be filled. And besides, nothing ever could fill it. Rather, I was already whole, emptying myself out, and I'd never needed to do that, either.

"It feels good to talk about him with you," he said. "I haven't talked about him like this in so long. I was always afraid that talking about him would kill me. But it actually feels like it's been waking me up, making me feel more alive."

"I'm glad." We locked into a gaze again, and I could see Gav. Sensitive, contemplative Gav. But I could also see a softer, gentler Garrett, one who perhaps was finally learning how to live with himself. "This has been fun," I said.

"Making music with you always is."

Where I normally would have heard flirtation, or

something shallow, instead I heard—and felt—something genuine, evidenced by the smile normally occupied by a smirk. Most days it took effort for Garrett to be genuine, because when he did, he was closer to himself, and to a truth he couldn't bear to face. But the way he'd just spoken…the words came authentically.

"This album…" I gushed. "When I first heard *Tapestry*, I knew I wanted to write good, timeless songs. But when I first heard *Fortune Tellers*, it was like a whole new world opened up. I wanted to make music that moved people not only figuratively but literally. I wanted to capture the sound of color. Of glitter. You know what a body of water looks like when the sun reflects off it? Like a thousand diamonds on the sea? That was *Fortune Tellers* for me. That's what I wanted for *Next Wave*. I wanted to do everything Taro was doing—you and Jon and Edgar. I wanted to impress you. All of you. Especially Gav. But you, too, Garrett."

Garrett didn't answer. Just sat there, next to me, with an expression of admiration coupled with appreciation, and I blushed.

"Sorry," I said sheepishly. "Fangirl came out."

"It's a pleasure to meet her," he replied softly. "That may be one of the nicest things anyone has ever said about our album and our music."

"Surely you've heard it before, especially from the fans."

"But to hear it from *you*, Johanna…with your enthusiasm. You should've seen your face. Glowing. And your eyes—dappling just like those diamonds on the sea."

A hot flash came over me. And yet, I highly doubted it was the product of age.

"You saw our vision at such a young age. You know that's what makes you special, right?" he said.

What was it that Rick had said about my being able tap into something that our male peers couldn't? Was that what made me special? Or was it something else, something more? Was it being *me* that made the difference?

I stared at Garrett, goggle-eyed. He looked as handsome as I'd seen him since the night of my birthday. He slowly, slightly leaned in. Like a fader being gently nudged forward. More bass, less high end. A mere fraction.

And yet, I pulled away, intuition seeming to say, *Not yet.* I hoped Garrett's intuition was telling him the same thing.

Returning my attention to the computer, I cleared my throat. "Let's punch up the last one," I said. I clicked on "The Crystal Ball." Without warning, a youthful, cheery voice filled the entire room. High-pitched. Impeccably British. Mischievous, even. As if he were standing right in front of us. "Can you try coming in on the backbeat, mate?"

My heart stopped before lodging itself in my throat.

I hadn't heard that voice in almost thirty years. Even digitally, he sounded so alive.

Gavin Chandler counted off the beats, pounded the kickdrum in a backbeat rhythm, then blew the tom-snare combo after the lead-in.

"Shit!" he said with a laugh.

That laugh. So full of heart and soul and youth.

An eighteen-year-old Garrett playfully chided him. "Get it right, you git, and maybe I'll join you." They laughed in unison. Two voices as one. Like doubling a vocal.

He counted off again, and this time got it right.

Garrett clicked Stop, reset the track to the beginning, and clicked Play.

We listened to Gav again. Two, three, four times. His was the only voice in the room.

Garrett slipped his hand into mine, our fingers interlocked, and we held on tight. Like plugging in to recharge a battery. I could feel the current moving from him to me and me to him.

"I'd almost forgotten what he sounded like, even though we're identical," he said barely above a whisper. "That laugh."

"I know," I whispered back.

We sat together, at the mixing desk, hands clasped, and we cried.

CHAPTER TWENTY-SIX

Garrett and I had gotten into a routine: Tennis in the morning; breakfast; jam in the studio (sometimes I played drums and he played piano, or I played piano and he played bass, and so on); dinner (we ate such a late breakfast that we often skipped lunch in favor of a snack); and classic movies at night. Not that we didn't occasionally spend time apart—a walk on the beach, a trip into town. But our time together was therapeutic. Garrett dug out old family photos and shared them with me—he and Gav dressed in matching soccer jerseys as kids, at their first school recital, posing in front of the Christmas tree with their parents, dressed in matching (and embarrassing) outfits of short pants and bow ties. They'd both started out as bowl-cut blonds with bangs that never quite stayed out of their eyes. Even as children they were handsome, precocious, little heartbreakers in training, as if they already knew their fate.

"My parents weren't the snapshot types," I said when Garrett asked if I had any to share. "And besides, I was a little butterball early on. I think they were as self-conscious of my body as I was.

"That's too bad," he said.

"In more ways than one."

He paused for a contemplative beat. "What made you finally lose the weight for good?"

"I think it was the same reason you finally decided to get sober. Life just got too depressing and unmanageable. I was winded climbing stairs. Perhaps my uncle's heart attack also had something to do with it, too. So I went to a nutritionist, bought a treadmill, and the rest is history."

"How did you resist booze and drugs?"

I shrugged. "They just didn't appeal to me. I was never even tempted."

"I envy that," he said. "So how do you cope when things are difficult?"

"I work my ass off. Or I hop on the treadmill. Down a glass of water. Bang my drums. I don't always make healthy food choices—kind of hard with our schedule, and I don't really like to cook for one—but I don't do the binge thing anymore, and I don't like the feeling of sitting for too long."

"I traveled a lot after I got sober," said Garrett. "Work reminded me too much of Gav, so keeping on the move seemed a better coping mechanism. After a while, however, I felt like I had no place else to go. These last few years… I've not coped very well. I haven't gotten drunk, but I've had little direction. Looking back, I think that's what all the traveling was about: direction. I was looking for someplace to go after Gav's death. Someplace to hide. I was looking for something to do. I think I'm still looking. I've never known myself as anything other than Gav's twin brother. Taro seemed to emphasize that."

I could relate.

"What's the hardest part about being you, Joey?" I chortled as Garrett caught himself. "I meant, what do you struggle with the most?"

"Loneliness," I replied, not missing a beat.

He seemed taken aback by this.

"I never felt lonely with your brother, though. Even when we were continents apart. Or this past year in the studio with you and the band."

Or these last few days with just you.

Garrett embraced me, and doing so released the invisible chokehold that had strangled me since childhood.

"You don't have to be alone anymore," he whispered.

"Neither do you," I whispered back.

That evening, after dinner, we watched the tribute *Concert for George Harrison* from 2002 at the Royal Albert Hall, both of us filled with longing to crawl inside the TV screen and grab an instrument.

"You know George was Gav's favorite Beatle," he said.

"George was everybody's favorite Beatle," I replied.

"I don't know, I've always been partial to Paul." He pointed at the stage on the screen, filled with legendary musicians of a generation that had escorted us into our lives and set the foundation for our art. "I'll bet you a million dollars that if our Gav had lived, he would've been right there, sitting at that kit next to Ringo's. He did phone George once. They had a nice chat. No doubt that with more time, they would've become friends."

I laughed. "That boy knew how to network."

"And how. If he didn't remain a drummer, he could've been either a talent scout or a manager of some other band."

"Nah," I said with a smile. "Gav was a producer through and through."

We watched Paul McCartney take the stage as the audience erupted in a collective yawp.

"So George was your favorite Beatle, too?" Garrett asked.

"I kind of rotated when it came to favorites. I wanted to be all of them," I said with a chuckle. "Story of my life. Each one of them had attributes I aspired to. Of course I love that Paul plays lefty. Like a kindred spirit." Then, after a beat, I confessed, "But I had a crush on George in *A Hard Day's Night*."

Garrett was amused. "Did you know the record company wanted Taro to make a movie like that?"

"I recall the rumors, yes."

"We all thought the idea was stupid. Never did get the right script. The worst one was some whodunit caper."

Garrett and I halted the conversation when the supergroup began to play "All Things Must Pass." We watched and listened, mesmerized. Paul's voice was soothing. Consoling, even. And, as music has the power to do, the message transcended time and space and people and spoke to only us at that precise moment. And as we sat, side by side, shoulder to shoulder, I could feel a wave of peace crest over us, as gentle as the ever-present surf outside. As if we'd never known it before, never understood it. As if we'd finally gotten the answer.

And somehow I knew it couldn't have happened at any other time or place or in anyone else's presence. Maybe George Harrison and Gavin Chandler had cosmically conspired to make it so.

The concert ended, and Garrett turned off the TV. The two of us sat in the dark, still and silent, save our breathing.

We found each other, eyes adjusting to the dark. Or perhaps, finding the light. Immersed in the now.

Garrett kissed me. Soft. Delicate. Precise.

I'd been so crazed with lust the last time we'd kissed, so starved for sex. But right then and there I was so clear-headed, mindful, aware. This kiss was like a beacon of light; it could guide me wherever I needed to go.

Not I—*we*. He was my friend, after all. But he was more than that.

I loved him.

We remained on the sofa and made out like two shy, nervous teenagers. We kissed and touched and curled into each other until we opened our eyes, locked our gaze, and a world of possibilities spilled over in our smiles.

We were a composition in progress, Garrett and me. A collection of instruments and harmonies, sharps and flats, arpeggios and codas and time changes. A melody and a rhythm. Notes on a page in splashes of ink that could be rewritten as many times as we wanted.

"Thank you," he said with a sigh.

We rose from the sofa, arm in arm, and went to bed.

The next morning, Garrett asked me to leave.

"Please don't mistake that as my usual dickish behavior or pushing you away," he beckoned. "Quite the opposite, actually. I feel as if I've woken up—like, *really* woken up—and I have so much to do, but I have to do it by myself now, you know what I mean?"

I'd never seen him so animated. I shared both his eagerness and his sense of purpose. "I do," I said, "and I couldn't agree with you more. It's time for me to go."

"A week," he said. "Give me one more week and we'll get back into the studio—*your* studio—and finish the album. I'm ready for it. God, I'm so ready. Or rather, I'm so close to being ready. I'll call the mates."

I was ready, too. For perhaps the first time in my life, I was ready for anything.

CHAPTER TWENTY-SEVEN

Ten days later, Johnny, Michael, Ian, and I reunited in my studio, waiting for Garrett to show up.

"This doesn't bode well," said Johnny. I'd called each of them and told them about the relapse when it had happened, and I knew Garrett had called them after I left.

"He's not the guy you last saw," I said. "You're all going to be pleasantly surprised." I hoped I was right.

"Do you know how close we are to this whole thing blowing up?" Ian said. "Janet's been keeping Sony on hold, but they may have already lost their patience. If they change their minds…"

"Then we independently release it," I said. "The crowdfunding is now four times what we projected. But look, we're not at that bridge. Just hang on. He'll be here."

Twenty minutes later, Garrett showed up dressed in new

clothes, clean-shaven, and his hair styled. You'd think he'd been on his way to an appearance on a late-night talk show than a band meeting.

But wow. He oozed style and charisma and sex appeal. A pop star through and through.

Not to mention how turned on I was.

Most important, he was more alive than I had seen him. *That's* what made him so attractive.

Armed with coffee, he distributed the cups and invited us to rearrange our chairs in a circle. The band meeting was officially underway.

"So it's time for me to make amends," he began after taking a deep breath. "Not just for the last few months, but the last thirty years."

He took another breath to compose himself.

"I'm sorry," he started. "I deprived you of your careers. I shut you out, I refused to share my grief over losing my brother—*our* brother—or to allow you to express yours around me. I'm sorry for years of bad behavior and empty apologies. But I've cleaned the slate and begun again. As of today, I'm fifteen days sober."

"Good for you," said Johnny. The others looked wary but attentive.

"I know I have a long way to go with each of you personally, and I'm going to work very hard on that, but I want to start over with the album, too."

Garrett must have seen the color drain from our faces, because he quickly added, "I don't mean throw everything out—I mean in attitude and approach and focus. I have a clear vision of what this album is now. I also want to play you some songs I've been working on all week, and I would like to add at least one of them to the album."

He asked Johnny for his acoustic guitar. Johnny reached

behind him and clasped it by the neck before gingerly passing it to Garrett. Garrett tuned it and began to play as he tapped his foot in four-four time, roughly the same tempo as "All Things Must Pass," and sang three verses and the chorus to a song he called "Brother Beyond." The song was simple in structure, yet melodic. The lyrics were more pathos than poetry, every word a heartstring.

It was about Gav. It was about Garrett. It was about me. Johnny. Ian. Michael.

And I knew that Laurel, or Cherry the barista, or anyone else who listened to it would believe unequivocally that it was about them, too.

We were in tears when he finished.

"God, mate, that hits you right here," said Ian, holding his hand over his heart.

"So freaking good," added Michael. "One of your best."

"Agreed," I said as I wiped my eyes and sniffled.

"Maybe you should take the lead vocal when we record it," said Ian.

Garrett grinned. "Thanks, but you know I can't sing for shit," he said with a laugh. "Even ol' Edgar couldn't save my voice." He repositioned his fingers on the fret board. "The next one is something Joey and I were playing around with. It's still a work in progress, though." He then played one of the songs we'd improvised during our jam sessions.

"That's got a good hook," said Johnny, who then reached for the electric guitar and picked up a riff that accentuated the hook even more. I grabbed my sticks and tapped out a rhythm on the back of the chair. Within sixty seconds we manned our instruments and learned the song. We had it down pat in three go-rounds, with Ian improvising lyrics and jotting them down along the way.

The change in each of us was apparent, and I think it took each of us by surprise equally. As if someone opened all the doors and windows and aired everything out. The room looked cleaner, smelled better, didn't feel quite so dense. We were full of energy, and not from the coffee.

We were alive.

"I know the story of this album, now," said Garrett. "It's *us*. All of us, including Johanna. We're coming back to each other. We're coming back from the brink of extinction and obscurity. We've come back to life. And we're going to make the best fucking comeback pop music has ever seen," he said, rallying us into a cheer.

CHAPTER TWENTY-EIGHT

We put the finishing touches to the album in Port Washington, and Rick and I co-mixed it. The final roster of songs—we even designated an A Side and B Side for the vinyl version—consisted of the following lineup:

Side A
Come Back
Shadows in the Sand
Don't Look Ahead
The Hampton Blues
Good Ol' Days

Side B
Edgar
I've Got You

Drummer Girl
Brother Beyond
One More

For the CD, we included three bonus tracks: "The Point of Power," "Say My Name," and a kick-ass remake of "Glossy" with Ian on vocals.

Every one of us was madly in love with the album, and we cried tears of joy as we all stood in the control booth and played the final mixes, start to finish. Rick was in love with it. Janet St. James was in love with it. Sony was in love with it.

"Once the single catches fire, the rest will follow," said Janet. "It's a matter of being uber-organized and getting an A-list marketing and publicity firm. Perform on both the morning and late-night shows. Snag a few cover stories. Do interviews with everyone—print, TV, radio, internet. I don't care if it's a college newspaper with three readers. And hit the podcasts."

"Taro, Taro, everywhere, just like the good ol' days," I said with a smile. "Tour England first."

"Definitely," said Michael.

A sly smile crossed Garrett's face. "You know what we should do? A gig at our old stomping grounds back home. Unannounced. Like the Beatles' rooftop concert. In fact, let's make that the video for 'Come Back.'"

"Brilliant," said Johnny and Ian in unison.

"Gav should somehow be represented, too," said Michael.

We all turned to Garrett, who looked wistfully at my drum kit, then said with a satisfied smile. "Yes, absolutely. I'd love that. So would he."

Then Garrett turned to me. "One more piece of business. Johanna, we've already had a meeting on this and we're all in agreement."

He took a breath before speaking, and then choked up as his eyes welled.

Oh my God, am I about to finally get canned?

"We want you to officially join Taro as our drummer."

My jaw dropped.

"You're a part of us now," said Garrett. "It was your vision, your musicianship, and your intelligence that made it into something that is simultaneously authentic to Taro and transcendent of Taro. No one else could've done it, and so successfully at that."

"You beat us back to life," said Michael.

"In every way possible," Ian added with a chuckle.

My body trembled as I spoke. "I'm speechless."

Garrett stood and faced me, his back to the others, and said softly, "You've got a family now, fucked up as it is."

I laughed through a blur of tears.

"What do you say, Paisley?" he asked, followed by a wink.

It was time to make peace with Paisley Parker, too. Not for an audience or an executive or an album or a memory. For *me*. Because she was me and I was her. And I loved her, I realized. I loved her more than anyone else.

And then, feeling as if I'd just swallowed sunshine, I grinned mischievously, picked up my sticks, sat at my kit, and clicked out four beats. "Gentlemen, let's have some fun."

EPILOGUE

Since the release of *Come Back*, Taro has been riding a wave of popularity that had far surpassed what we'd pragmatically predicted. The album went to number one on the *Billboard* chart and number one on iTunes and was nominated for a host of Grammys, including Best Album, Best Producer, and Best Single for "Come Back." "Brother Beyond" was the second single; it had already gotten a head start from eager DJs and iTunes analytics showing it as one of the most frequently downloaded songs.

The fans have been positively electric. What's more, a number of teens still filled out the crowd—this time the sons and daughters of original Taro fans. And their husbands. And friends. And siblings. It's a party of past and future, old and new memories. I don't know what's been more fun—to see the delight on their faces or on Ian's from the moment we take the stage until we leave.

Better yet, we're tight. We're five musicians who know each other so well, we can read each other's minds. Especially Garrett and me. He once described Gav and me as "two peas in a pod." Garrett and I were more like chocolate and peanut butter—better combined than solo. As he'd watch me for time changes, count-offs, and cut-offs, he'd burst into a grin—the smirk long gone—a topaz sparkle of unbridled joy in his eyes. As if we shared a secret despite everyone being in on it. And at the end of every performance of "Last Call," he would mouth to me: *I love all of you.* To which I would give one of my sticks a charismatic twirl, point it at him, and reply: *Love-all.* In tennis, Love-all is the starting point. Both players are in equal standing, and the possibilities are endless.

The guys dressed in high-fashion print shirts and tight jeans and boots, a look that went over well on the Taro album cover, especially the vinyl version. The four of them in their hometown, posed, a drumkit in the background to honor who was simultaneously absent and present. We'd decided to keep me off the cover—I didn't want to be seen as a replacement for Gav. For the tour, however, I complemented the guys' look with ripped jeans and boots; in lieu of my signature scarf, I opted for a custom designed Punk Masters black T-shirt with PAISLEY emblazoned in a neon-pink font. I had never imagined it would feel like a homecoming, or that it would feel so good.

On this particular night at Radio City Music Hall, Ian took a break from the set list after "Brother Beyond," which was just as much a fan favorite live as the recorded version.

"Today, we're here to celebrate a special birthday," Ian said. The crowd cheered. They knew. But of course, Ian filled in the details for the new fans. "Our Garrett Chandler," he said as he gestured to his right. The spotlight went on Garrett, who took a humble bow. "In what has become a Taro tradition, we're going to sing a little song for him, and for someone equally special whom we love and miss."

Garrett gawked at Ian as the surprise slowly registered, and he transformed from befuddled to bedazzled.

I counted off the beats and Michael broke into The Beatles' "Birthday." (Key of A, of course.) We all sang this time, replacing the lyric "it's my birthday, too" to "it's Gav's birthday, too" as a photo of the young identical twins—adorned with matching punk haircuts and David Bowie T-shirts—appeared on the monstrous video screen above us. The audience wooted and cheered, and from behind my kit I witnessed Garrett basking in the moment while simultaneously missing his brother so damn much it squeezed his heart.

Except this time he didn't cry alone. We finished the song as the audience clapped to the beat, and at the outro all occupants of Radio City Music Hall were verklempt, collectively full of joy and heartbreak.

That was how life worked now, especially for Garrett and me. And it was OK. It had become something we had acclimated to. It was even comforting at times, because it was no longer something to be caged separately, the joy or the heartbreak. They were allowed to peacefully coexist in the open, and they did.

Ian sidled to Garrett when we finished the song and hugged him hard. "We love you," said Ian. The audience offered up a cheer of affirmation.

Garrett took Ian's mic. "*We* love you," he said, giving each of his bandmates a nod. He faced the crowd. "And we love *you*," he shouted, stirring up the crowd again. "My brother loved you all so much, and he's here—I know he's here right now, and he's so grateful."

With that, Ian reclaimed the mic and introduced the next song: “It’s time for another classic”—cheers—“featuring our new drummer, Johanna Paisley Parker.” He bowed to me as he included the middle name. He did it every time, and every time I twirled my stick like a baton and tossed it the air. A photo of sixteen-year-old me appeared on the screen, and the audience welcomed it, and *me*, as the spotlight shone on my kit.

For “Glossy,” Ian and I switched off the verses and doubled on the chorus, with a hard beat and more of a rock edge than the original. The audience loved it. We played it at every show, and I didn’t get sick of it once.

ACKNOWLEDGMENTS AND A NOTE FROM THE AUTHOR

I began writing this novel in 2014, hit the wall at about 35,000 words, and put it down with the intention of picking it back up way, way sooner than I did.

But things happened: I made one of several future moves that same year. I was contracted to write *Pasta Wars*, and then two more books—and although I'd pitched this manuscript as one of those two books, the publisher rejected it.

More big life changes: I got married. Moved across the country several times. My husband and I cowrote and published *You, Me & Mr. Blue Sky*. Our publisher dropped us. My magical ride of success concluded in a series of commercial flops. I lost my confidence. And although I still loved this manuscript, this story and these characters, I feared its time had passed.

Fast-forward to the end of 2020, when I took a three-month social media hiatus and decided to find out if this story could be salvaged.

It could. And I was more in love with it than ever.

And yet, it still had a long road ahead to go through the submission process during a time when the publishing industry, like so many other industries, was still trying to rebound from the effects of the pandemic. In the end, those submissions didn't pan out. But I have never lost my fervent belief in this book.

And so, dear reader, it has finally been born into the world, into your hands and heart, and for that I am most grateful.

Of course, even though writing is a solitary act, it still takes a village to birth a book. Here are a handful of those people who helped make this possible:

Nalini Akolekar had every reason in the world to cut me loose and never did. She believed in this book as much as I did and went to bat at every turn for it.

Mike Lorello welcomed me into his studio not as his sister but as an observer. He showed me the ropes, assisted me with terminology and tools, and gave me the highest praise possible when he said I nailed the experience and characterization of a professional producer, engineer, and musician. Rest assured, he is one of Joey's idols and inspirations as much as he is mine.

The rest of my siblings: Bobby, Rich, Steve, Mary, and Paul, my wombmate, have also awed me with their musical talent and inventiveness. What a gift to grow up among them.

Bryony Evans, Maureen Bensa, and Karen Booth read the manuscript in an early incarnation, and helped me make it better as a result. Chrissy Wiley gave me the lowdown on Paul McCartney's Rickenbacker.

Tiffany Yates Martin did not work with me in a professional capacity on this book, but rest assured she was all over it in the best way possible, and she doesn't even know it.

Andrew "Durandy" Golub, David Orwick, Patty Palazzo,

Morgan Richter, Dana Gierdowski, Katherine Berry, Kelly Hewins, Kelly Sutphin, Lisa Schlossberg, and Elisa DiLeo are just a few who would and should be Taro fans. Their friendship, support, and Duranie fellowship has been a gift. And Annie Zaleski unknowingly raised the bar. I hope I cleared it.

My Lorello, Mottola, and Clines families' faith in me carried me during a time when I had little faith in myself.

My uncle Ronnie Mottola was one of the very first readers of my novel *Faking It*, and even arranged for the renowned Junior's Restaurant in New York to send me a complimentary cheesecake for my 40th birthday. A collector of guitars and a lover of great music—especially classic rock—whenever I lamented that I couldn't play guitar as well as my siblings, he encouraged me to play for the joy and not worry about the precision. And he cheered the loudest when I successfully strummed my first barre chord. Moreover, he was a musician in his own right, full of talent and modesty. He would have loved Joey Parker. Heck, he probably would have appreciated Taro, too. Perhaps he's with Gav, keeping the beat, watching over me and this book. I sure do miss him. And, like Joey's Uncle Oscar, we lost him way too soon.

My father, Michael Lorello Sr., also did not live to see this book come to fruition. If there's an object that defines my dad, it's his 1944 Epiphone Spartan acoustic guitar. One strum is still sublime. He knew his way around a guitar. He loved Mel Tormé and Joe Pass and instilled a love of Ella Fitzgerald in me. He also loved the Beatles. Throughout his life he bragged about his children's musical talent, and even gave his youngest daughter a couple of lessons. I know he was proud of me.

My mother, Eda Lorello. I don't even have the words to aptly describe the monumental role she's played throughout my life.

My cat, Spatz. "She's my Rushmore, Max."

Fretless the dog kept my husband company while I worked.

Readers, fellow authors, and friends. They're the reason why I want to keep writing and publishing books. Gratitude especially to those who've stuck by me since day one, and especially through the drought.

And of course, my dearest Craig. He's given so much of his time and talent so that I can do what my heart desires. He's responsible for the production of this book. He's the bass to my beat.

If I have left anyone out, please accept my sincere apology.

Finally, you may have noticed that a certain band was conspicuously absent from this novel. In Taro's world, Duran Duran could not have co-existed (although I couldn't resist Joey and Taro jamming to a Power Station song)—and yet, they loomed large and were on every page—between the notes, if you will, which was in the running for the novel's title. I suppose it's no surprise that the title I ultimately chose is also a song from their 2021 album *Future Past*. For forty years and counting, Duran Duran have inspired, uplifted, and consoled me during the best and worst of times. They have endured as the soundtrack of my life and the lens of my world. No doubt they will do it for as long as they and I live. What better real-life epilogue to this book than to witness their induction into the Rock & Roll Hall of Fame. I couldn't be a prouder fan.

Likewise, the many bands and artists mentioned in this book (and many that weren't) have also defined and inspired me to be the best at what I do, keeping this heaven alive.

Thank you, dear reader, for being with me and spending time in this world.

Elisa
June 2022

ABOUT THE AUTHOR

Elisa Lorello is the bestselling author of eleven novels and one memoir. The youngest of seven, she grew up on Long Island and graduated with two degrees from University of Massachusetts-Dartmouth. Since 2010 she's sold over a half-million units worldwide and has been featured in the *Charlotte Observer*, *Woman's World* magazine, *Rachel Ray Every Day* magazine, *Montana Quarterly*, *Writer's Digest* Online, and Jane Friedman's *Five On* blog series. She's also been a guest on multiple podcasts, a featured speaker at libraries and schools, and a panelist at the Book Expo of America.

Elisa is a lifelong Duran Duran fan and a proud Gen-Xer, can sing two-part harmony, and devours chocolate chip cookies (not always at the same time). She currently lives in Montana with her husband (bestselling author Craig Lancaster) and their two pets.

Did you enjoy All of You*? Please leave a review on your favorite book review site, and/or share it with your friends on social media!*

CONNECT WITH ELISA LORELLO

- Subscribe to Elisa's weekly newsletter (which she loves to write) and learn more about Elisa at www.elisalorello.com.
- Follow Elisa on BookBub.
- Follow Elisa on Twitter (@elisalorello), Instagram (@elisalorello), and Facebook (Elisa Lorello, Author).

ALSO...

- Listen to Mike Lorello's music at www.themikelorelloproject.com.
- Learn more about Duran Duran at www.duranduran.com.
- Check out *The D Side* podcast wherever you listen to podcasts.
- Shop for Punk Masters T-shirts at www.punkmasters.com.